Designs by Isabelle

BY LAURENCE YEP

*To Peter Brosius of the Children's Theatre Company and especially to
the Dragon King, David Furumoto, who danced on stilts*

Published by American Girl Publishing
Copyright © 2014 American Girl

Questions or comments? Call 1-800-845-0005, visit **americangirl.com**, or write to
Customer Service, American Girl, 8400 Fairway Place, Middleton, WI 53562-0497.

Printed in China
14 15 16 17 18 19 20 21 LEO 10 9 8 7 6 5 4 3 2 1

All American Girl marks and Isabelle™ are trademarks of American Girl.

This book is a work of fiction. Any similarity to real persons, living or dead, is coincidental
and not intended by American Girl. References to real events, people, or places are used
fictitiously. Other names, characters, places, and incidents are the products of imagination.

Illustrations by Anna Kmet

Special thanks to Kristy Callaway, executive director of Arts Schools Network;
and Shannon Gallagher, owner of and instructor at Premier Dance Academy, LLC,
Madison, WI

Cataloging-in-Publication Data available from the Library of Congress.

Contents

CHAPTER 1

The Mouse Whisperer

On Saturday, our break was almost over, and the other dancers had already gone back inside the studio. But I wanted to visualize my routine one more time to smooth out a few tricky parts, so I hung back in the hallway.

I was on the second floor of the Hart Dance Company, the HDC, surrounded by rehearsal studios. Beneath my feet, on the street level, was the large theater where my big sister, Jade, and I would dance *The Nutcracker* in just a few short weeks. My stomach fluttered at the thought.

Through the hallway window, I caught sight of someone in a giant turkey costume standing on the street corner. On top of the turkey's head was a Santa hat, and the turkey was waving a large sign advertising a pre-Christmas sale.

Thanksgiving was still a couple of weeks off, but the holiday season had already started for my family. Dad's band was getting gigs for company parties, and Mom was busy selling her fabric art at holiday craft fairs. Normally I loved the holidays, but this year I was too busy preparing for *The Nutcracker* to enjoy them.

Stay focused, I told myself, turning away from the window. I began my visualization again, picturing in my mind a big chest full of toys. Each toy was part of my dance routine, and as I picked up the first one, a jack-in-the-box, I moved my arms and legs slightly and imagined popping into the air like a jester coming out of a box.

Then, in my mind, I set aside the jack-in-the-box and pulled a toy top out of the chest.

As I readied my feet, I said to myself, *Spin.*

I visualized myself spinning like a top, faster and faster.

Suddenly I heard a little girl crying from down the hall. "I'm stuck!" she screeched.

I jogged down the hall and found three kids in mouse costumes standing in front of the restroom. One of them was hopping up and down and waving her paws in the air. "I'm stuck! I'm stuck!" she wailed from inside the big mouse head. Judging by her height, I guessed she was only about five years old.

"We'll fix it, Addison," the second mouse promised. "Just hold still."

"Can I help?" I asked.

"The zipper is jammed," grunted the third mouse. Her big, clumsy paw was having trouble holding on to the tab of Addison's zipper.

"Don't worry," I said, trying to calm Addison.

2

"I'm an expert at zippers." At least I'd watched my mother sew enough of them onto clothes.

Addison dropped her paws to her sides, and the third mouse stepped back so that I could inspect the zipper. Just as I had thought, some material had gotten caught in the zipper. I worked the zipper upward until the teeth let go of the fabric. Then I slowly eased the zipper down, revealing the back of Addison's T-shirt.

"There you go," I said, lifting up the mouse head. Addison's red hair was matted down with sweat. It must have been hot inside the head.

Addison's freckles wriggled when she said, "Hurry."

As soon as her two friends helped her out of her mouse suit, she raced into the restroom.

"Are you on a break, too?" I asked the remaining mice.

When they took off their mouse heads, I saw two more little girls: a tall, thin Asian girl and a brunette with rosy round cheeks, who answered me eagerly. "We just came along to help Addison out of her costume," she explained.

"I was glad to get away," the taller girl added. "I hate imp—, imp—"

The rosy-cheeked girl tried her hand at saying the strange word, too. "Im-per-fizzing," she sounded out. "We're supposed to play like mice, but we don't do it good enough for Mr. Kosloff."

I made a guess at what Mr. Kosloff was asking them to do. "My modern dance teacher makes us *improvise*, or make up new dance moves, a lot," I told them. "One time I even had to dance like a needle."

Whether I was improvising or just practicing a dance move, it helped to picture images in my head—like the toys in a toy chest. Maybe something like that could help these little mice, too.

But how would I visualize a mouse having fun? I wondered. Then my favorite picture book popped into my head. It was about the three blind mice. *Those* were mice who knew how to have a good time.

"You could try dancing like the three blind mice," I suggested, just as Addison came out of the restroom.

"Would you show us?" asked the tallest mouse.

"Please!" begged the girl with brown hair.

I should have gone back to rehearsal, but I couldn't resist showing off a little. "Okay," I said. "But first let's get you back to your studio." After

4

helping Addison zip up into her suit, we hurried down the hallway.

The tallest mouse led us toward Studio B, and I glanced through the open doorway. I saw a dozen more mice of all sizes running around. At the back of the studio, I saw a young blonde woman with a pony-tail and glasses talking to the director, Mr. Kosloff.

He was a chubby man who kept his beard neatly trimmed and his head shaved. At auditions for *The Nutcracker,* he had seemed strict and unfriendly—especially when he was dismissing dancers who didn't make the cut. So even though he had chosen me for his cast, I still felt a little uneasy around him.

"Okay, I think I'd do something like this," I murmured to Addison and her friends, pausing just outside the studio door. I opened the *Three Blind Mice* picture book in my memory and imagined I was entering the farmer's house.

I'm not scared of the farmer or his wife, I told myself. *But how do I show that without using words?* I began to sway my head from side to side as if I owned the world. Then, planting my fists on my hips, I began to dance strutting steps around Addison and her friends.

Stopping after a minute, I said encouragingly,

"Now you three try it."

The little mice stumbled at first, but as they got into their roles, they really began to strut.

"That's great!" I said. I caught Addison's shoulder and aimed her toward Studio B. "Now show those other mice what real fun looks like."

"Yes, this is *it*! Mice with attitude," I heard a man say. When I glanced back at the doorway, I saw Mr. Kosloff and the blonde-haired woman standing there watching the three little mice. "In fact, let's have *all* the mice swagger like that."

The blonde woman mouthed a "thank you" to me and then turned to Mr. Kosloff. "I knew the old mouse costumes would get them into character," she said, winking at me. She stepped aside to let Addison and her friends back into the studio.

"I'm counting on you, Bettina," Mr. Kosloff said to her as he stepped out into the hallway and closed the door.

I wasn't sure if he had seen me talking with Addison and her friends. Just in case, I scooted back toward my rehearsal room, Studio C, before he thought I was goofing off when I should have been practicing.

Too late. "Wait a moment," he said.

I turned around nervously, expecting him to scold me.

"You're my little Gingerbread Girl," he said, his fingers tapping his lower lip. "Let's see . . . Isabelle . . . Isabelle?"

"Isabelle Palmer, sir," I said.

"Yes, Jade's sister, Isabelle," he said with a smile.

It was amazing that Mr. Kosloff remembered my first name. Jade was such a great dancer that usually I was known just as "Jade's little sister."

Mr. Kosloff's forehead wrinkled as he asked, "Shouldn't you be rehearsing right now?"

I gulped. "Ms. Ferri let us take a break," I quickly explained.

"Well, you're very good with children," Mr. Kosloff said. "Do you have younger sisters and brothers?"

"No, sir," I said. "But my dad works at a hospital. He likes to visit the children's ward, and sometimes I've gone with him to play with the kids. We bring old costumes and props for the kids to use."

"Costumes, eh?" he asked. "I liked your costume in the Autumn Festival. Did your mother design it?"

I couldn't believe Mr. Kosloff had noticed my "waltzing flower" costume, let alone remembered it. "No, sir," I said, with a hint of pride. "I designed the costume, but my mom sewed it for me."

"Well, you both did a very good job," said Mr. Kosloff kindly.

Now that I was talking face to face with Mr. Kosloff, he actually seemed sort of nice.

He thought for a moment and then asked, "Would you do me a favor?"

I couldn't think of what Mr. Kosloff might possibly need my help with, but I said, "Sure."

"The party in Act One is set in modern times, but I'm not up on the latest styles for young people, so I'm a little worried about the designs for the children's costumes," he said. "Would you be willing to give me your opinion?"

I hesitated, feeling another rush of nervousness. "Um, sure," I said finally, "but I'm not an expert, Mr. Kosloff."

"You're more of an expert than I am at being a kid," he said. "The wardrobe department on the third floor has the designs. Ask for Margie."

I was feeling a little dazed. "Third floor," I repeated.

"I'll tell Margie to make copies of the designs for you, and you can pick them up after rehearsal. Now if you'll excuse me, I have to get back to your sister's group," he said, motioning toward Studio A. "And you have to get back to Ms. Ferri." He winked. "I know you'll knock 'em dead."

As soon as Mr. Kosloff walked away, I had to fight the urge to rush up to the third floor to see the costumes. I was itching to see what Jade was going to wear in her role as Clara. If I hadn't had castmates waiting for me in Studio C, I would have dashed up those stairs in a heartbeat.

But instead, I was good and went back into my studio. *So Santa can keep me off his naughty list this year,* I thought with a sigh—and a smile.

CHAPTER 2

Bowling-Ball Belle

As I hurried back into Studio C, I found my dance teacher, Ms. Ferri, sitting in a chair, adjusting the straps on a pair of stilts. Ms. Ferri was a tall woman in her fifties with frizzy brown hair. She had risen to principal dancer at the HDC, so she had danced some of the most important roles. Then, after retiring from dancing, she'd become the ballet mistress at HDC.

Ms. Ferri was so nice that I couldn't help wishing she taught ballet at my school, Anna Hart School of the Arts, so that I could have her all week instead of just on the weekends. But Ms. Ferri was too busy conducting the daily class for the HDC's professional dancers. And this year, she was busy rehearsing her own role in *The Nutcracker*, too—the role of Mother Ginger.

Ms. Ferri's stilts were made out of metal rods about a yard high. In New York City Ballet's version of *The Nutcracker*, men played Mother Ginger because the costume was so big and heavy. But Ms. Ferri was tall and strong enough to handle it. After years of playing Mother Ginger, she was a pro at managing the costume's weight while she walked on stilts. No one would see the stilts, because she'd wear a skirt big enough to hide them—plus eight kids.

Ms. Ferri glanced my way when she heard the door to the studio close behind me. "Where have you been, Isabelle?" she asked, but she didn't wait for me to answer. Instead, she turned to the other seven boys and girls in the studio. "Places, everyone. I want to run through the complete dance, so no matter what happens, keep going, okay?"

Bracing her hand against the wall, she carefully rose on her stilts until she towered above us. All eight of us gathered around her. Except for Luisa and Renata, I didn't know the other dancers, because they came from other schools.

Luisa was my best friend and went with me to Anna Hart. Renata went to school with us, too, but she and I got along like cats and dogs. It didn't help that I had beat her out for the role of Gingerbread Girl in *The Nutcracker*. Renata had been cast in another role, but she was my understudy. That meant that if anything happened to me, she would play my part. And I could tell by the way she looked at me during rehearsals, she was pretty much hoping something *would* happen to me.

I tried not to think about that as I stood shoulder to shoulder with Luisa and Renata in front of Ms. Ferri. More castmates lined up behind her until we formed a ring around her. Then we all hunched forward, our hands on our knees as if we were in a low tunnel. It was the opposite of all the graceful ballet positions we had learned, but it was the only way we could fit inside the big costume skirt that Ms. Ferri would wear as Mother Ginger.

When we had begun rehearsals two weekends ago, I had assumed we would practice the scenes in order. Instead, we had been split into groups that rehearsed at the same time in different studios. While I was practicing my routine in Act Two, my sister, Jade, was learning to be Clara in Act One. It was like making the individual beads separately and then later stringing them together in order for the final production.

The Nutcracker begins with a Christmas Eve party. A girl, Clara, receives the Nutcracker—a soldier carved from wood—as a gift. Put a nut in its mouth and move a handle, and the nutshell is broken so that you can get the nut inside.

After the party ends, Clara goes to the living room to get the Nutcracker, which has suddenly come to life. She finds the Nutcracker and toy soldiers fighting an army of mice. Clara throws a slipper at the Mouse King, who turns to see who threw it. And the

Nutcracker kills the distracted mouse and shows his true form, a prince.

In the original production, the prince then takes Clara to the Land of Sweets, where there are all sorts of entertainments in her honor. But this year Mr. Kosloff was creating a brand-new version, so the prince was going to take Clara to the Land of Dreams instead. That would let Mr. Kosloff blend in short fairy-tale dances, like the "Runaway Gingerbread Cookie," with audience favorites from the old version, like the "Dance of the Sugar Plum Fairy," while the prince and Clara watched.

The gingerbread cookie part was where I came in. Mother Ginger baked a cookie—me—who ran away. I had to leap out from Mother Ginger's giant skirt, and my castmates were going to be different characters trying to catch me.

"Claude, if you please," Ms. Ferri said, motioning to the rehearsal pianist.

Claude, a music student at George Washington University, was so tall and thin, he looked as if he were made of toothpicks. As he started playing the piano, Ms. Ferri began to keep count by clapping her hands. From the corner of my eye, I saw Luisa's lips moving as she kept count, too. On the fourth count, Ms. Ferri began stamping her feet. I was used to the metallic *thud* of her stilts by now. When she'd done that four times, she announced, *"And we begin."*

She stepped toward her right, and when her left foot joined her right, the rest of us took a step to the side—all of us keeping our strides about the same length. When we brought our feet together again, she took another sideways step in time to the music. If someone had peeked into the studio, they would have thought we were baby crabs out for a walk with our mother.

During the first rehearsal, my castmates and I had tripped over one another, and there had been a lot of kicked shins and stomped-on toes. But after two weeks, we were synchronizing into a smooth unit.

Finally, we reached that point in the music when Ms. Ferri stopped. "We have landed," she announced. "And up goes the skirt panel. And out goes Isabelle."

This was it—the moment I'd been waiting for. As I took a couple of steps through the imaginary opening in the skirt, I pictured that big chest of toys. The one right on top was a jack-in-the-box. I sprang straight up into a *jeté*, imagining a child shrieking happily.

Kicking off on my left foot, I swept my right foot in front of me. At the same time, I brought my arms down so that my hands were inches from my legs and raised them in front of my waist.

When I landed, I put my legs together and arched my back.

"Great acting, Isabelle," Ms. Ferri said encouragingly. "Keep doing what you're doing."

The compliment made my heart leap. So far I'd managed to do everything pretty well. I was determined to do the rest exactly right and prove to Ms. Ferri—and to Renata—that I deserved this role.

When Ms. Ferri, as Mother Ginger, began waving for me to come back to her, this Gingerbread Girl shook her head and jumped away.

"Put up your arms when you land!" Ms. Ferri instructed as she shot her own arms up into the air. "And remember to celebrate! Hooray for the Fourth of July! Merry Christmas! Happy Arbor Day!"

So the next time I landed after a jump, I raised my arms and grinned as if I were enjoying every holiday rolled into one. I began to move away in a series of leaps along a broad, curving path. As I circled counter-clockwise around the room, the others danced away from Ms. Ferri in a clockwise direction.

Each of them stopped at different places. They were the characters who were supposed to try to catch me.

The first up was Emilio, playing the part of a police officer. When he spotted me, he rubbed his stomach as if he were starving and tried to grab me. I was supposed to pirouette away from him.

I'd been practicing pirouettes for years, but lately I'd been having trouble with them sometimes. As I pictured the spinning toy top, I positioned my feet carefully. *Spin,* I told myself.

I rose on the ball of my right foot with my left leg bent and began to turn. I wobbled a little as I spun away from Emilio, but it was so slight that I hoped no one noticed.

The next character was a freckle-faced dancer named Agnes playing the role of a milkmaid. She rubbed her stomach hungrily just as Emilio had done and then stretched out her arms.

This time I was determined to get my pirouette perfect. I ran through all the steps—beginning with finding a spot on the wall. Each time I finished my spin, I stared at that same point to keep from getting too dizzy. But I was so busy running through my list of steps that I forgot to smile.

"Don't look so grim, Isabelle," Ms. Ferri

instructed. "Feel the joy."

I pulled the corners of my mouth up into what I hoped was a grin, but it probably would have scared small children.

Whirl like a top, I told myself.

Raising my left leg again, I began to turn. Though I tried my best, I felt myself tilt ever so slightly. Agnes's hands twitched as if she was getting ready to steady me.

She wasn't the only one who'd noticed. Renata, playing the role of a duchess, was my next stop. As she rubbed her stomach, she whispered, "How'd you get this role, Dizzy Izzy? It should've been mine."

I'll show you who should be the Gingerbread Girl, I retorted in my mind. As I started my third pirouette, I decided that I must have been going too slow with Agnes. *Spin faster,* I told myself. But I immediately lost my balance again and fell right into Renata's arms. She seemed just as disgusted by that as I was.

"Catch and release, Renata," Ms. Ferri ordered.

With a smirk, Renata pushed me away. "What are you supposed to be, anyway?" she asked. "A human bowling ball?"

I heard giggles from some of the nearby dancers. Renata's teasing wasn't going to improve my

17

pirouettes. What was I doing wrong?

I managed to get through my pirouettes with the next three castmates, but if I'd been graded on those spins, I wouldn't have scored over a C+. By the time I reached Luisa—the seventh and last dancer who was supposed to catch me—I decided that *this* pirouette was going to be the spin of spins.

Luisa stood with her legs crossed, smiling slyly. Her character—a fox—was supposed to ignore me, but she gave me a little nod to encourage me. Then she deliberately looked away.

I danced all around her, trying to get her to notice me. When she lunged forward to snatch me, I tried to pirouette away. But again I lost control and would have crash-landed if she hadn't caught me.

"Upsy-daisy," she whispered as she shoved me back onto my feet.

Ms. Ferri held out her arms and fluttered her fingers. "All of you, come to Mama," she said.

But I'd thrown off the others' timing as well as my own, and the music ended before we could reach Ms. Ferri. I shuffled to a stop with the others.

Ms. Ferri scratched her nose. "Well," she said and then repeated more slowly, "wel-l-l, this is what practices are for: to work out the mistakes." Was she looking right at me when she said that? I was pretty sure she was.

Renata deliberately bumped me as we returned to our original spots to try the routine again. "Watch your step this time, Bowling-Ball Belle," she whispered.

I fought the wave of anger rising in my chest. Why did Renata have to be in this cast? She wouldn't be happy until she had my role. That made me more determined than ever to perfect my pirouettes.

At first I'd thought that Mr. Kosloff had made a mistake when he had cast me for such a big part, but now that it was mine, I didn't intend to give it up. Not to Renata. Not to *anyone*. I found my place next to Luisa and squared my shoulders.

CHAPTER 3
The Real Fairy Godmother

I was glad when rehearsals finally ended. I had wobbled my way through the rest of my pirouettes, and I just couldn't figure out why.

As we bent over to get our bags, I grumbled softly to Luisa, "I'd like to wipe that smirk right off Renata's face."

Luisa whispered, "Don't pay any attention to Renata. She's just jealous."

I glanced at the corner where a smiling Renata was chatting with Ms. Ferri. Maybe she was asking a genuine question, or maybe she was buttering up our instructor, trying to steal my part.

"Can you see what I'm doing wrong with my pirouettes?" I asked Luisa, hoping for any pointers I could get.

"No," she admitted, "but maybe Jade can figure it out."

"Yeah, maybe," I said. But lately, Jade was barely talking to me, or to anyone. I figured she was concentrating on her big role as Clara. I'd have to wait for the right moment to ask her for help with my own dancing.

As we headed toward the doorway, Luisa took out her phone and checked her voicemails. The next moment, she gave a little skip and said, "Danny left a message!" Danny, her older brother, had joined the army last summer.

"What did he say?" I asked.

Luisa threw an arm around me and gave me a hug. "He's coming to our show!" she said happily. "He's got leave."

"That's great!" I said. "He'll love seeing you." I'd be happy to see Danny again, too. But then I suddenly wondered, *Will he watch* me *perform as the Gingerbread Girl—or Renata?*

As we stepped out into the hallway, the door to Studio A opened and several dancers came out, including Jade. Her blonde hair was still pulled up into a perfect bun, but she looked tired.

"Hey, how did it go?" I asked.

She shrugged. "Okay, I guess," she mumbled.

My sister never liked to brag, but today her shoulders were hunched and her lips were pressed tight. Usually she was so excited about a dance routine. When it came to ballet, there wasn't anything she couldn't do. "Just okay?" I pressed.

"Clara's a big role," Jade said. "I've got a lot to remember."

"She's the heart of the show," Luisa agreed sympathetically.

I couldn't blame my sister for worrying a little. She had been practicing her role hour after hour at home. So even though I would have liked to ask for her advice about my routine, I decided to wait until later.

"Ready to go?" Luisa asked.

"I've got an errand to run on the third floor before we go," I said.

I had been feeling frustrated by those pesky pirouettes, but when I thought about the costumes, excitement and curiosity took over. There were three casts for *The Nutcracker,* and the HDC's wardrobe department turned out costumes for all of them. I couldn't wait to see how they did it.

"What's up there?" Luisa asked as she fell into step beside me.

I tried to answer matter-of-factly. "Mr. Kosloff wanted me to look at some of the costumes for the children's party scene," I said.

Luisa punched my shoulder playfully. "Next time, share the good news, girl," she said with a grin. "If I'd been asked to do something like that, *everyone* would have heard about it by now."

"Yeah, congratulations," Jade murmured. She knew how much I loved costume design—and how exciting this must be for me—so I expected more of a reaction from her. But I guess it was just another sign that her mind was busy with other things.

We went up the stairs to the third floor and into a small lounge with mismatched sofas. Hanging on the wall were large posters of the theater's shows and some black-and-white photos of dancers caught mid-jump.

"I think this is where the company members hang out," Jade said.

We walked through the lounge and down the corridor to a door with a sign that read "Wardrobe."

When I opened the door, I felt as if I were stepping into a cave filled with treasure, like the one in the story "Ali Baba and the Forty Thieves." Only instead of chests of gold coins and jewels, there was a whole wall filled with bolts of fabric in all sorts of colors and patterns. The shelves were lined with bins of feathers, fake fur, buttons, lace, and trimmings. I wanted to stroke every fabric and feel each object. Was it soft? Did it shine? How would I mix and match these things? I could spend the rest of my life coming up with designs using all of this stuff.

A long table near the door held pieces of cut fabric, and my fingers itched to put them together like parts of a puzzle. Instead, I gazed past the table and noticed several people working in the room. One woman fluffed the layers of a tutu hanging on a dress form. From a clothesline above her head, pancake tutus—short skirts with stiff layers of chiffon, tulle, and organdy—hung like frilly flying saucers.

When I heard the familiar *burr* of sewing machines, I glanced at a woman and a man hunched over two machines, carefully sewing fancy costumes of embroidered cloth. More costumes dangled from clotheslines over their heads, looking like brightly colored parrots roosting near the ceiling.

At another table with a small, bright lamp, a woman sewed what looked like sequins onto the bodice of a costume. Behind her, a man was busy making a tall, bulb-shaped soldier's hat out of black fake fur.

I jumped when a middle-aged brunette woman asked, "May I help you?"

Her sweatshirt was covered with little bits of different-colored thread and lint. It reminded me of Mom's clothes after she finished cutting and sewing one of her creations. The woman was holding a cup labeled with the words "The Real Fairy Godmother." The string of a tea bag dangled over the side.

I recognized this woman as the seamstress who had taken our measurements after our first rehearsal, but I didn't know her name. "Um, hi," I said. "Mr. Kosloff said he'd have some copies of his costume designs for me. May I speak with Margie, please?"

The woman sipped her tea noisily. "Isabelle Palmer, right?" she asked.

"Yes, ma'am," I said.

"Hi, I'm Margie," she said warmly. "Mr. Kosloff said you'd be coming up." She looked at me curiously and added, "You're a little younger than I thought you'd be."

"You should've seen the great costumes she designed for our school show," Luisa bragged.

Margie nodded knowingly. "You're drooling like my little boy when I take him into a candy store," she said with a smile.

She was right. I spread my arms as if I could somehow hug the whole room. "This place is amazing," I said.

Margie seemed pleased. "Cinderella's godmother has got nothing on us," she joked. "And our gowns last past midnight." She picked up a large brown envelope from a desk and handed it to me.

25

"Here. I printed out copies of the designs that
Mr. Kosloff wanted you to take a look at."

"Thanks," I said, holding my breath as I took
the envelope. Was this really happening?

Luisa seemed as excited as I was. As soon as
we were in the hallway again, she reached for the
envelope. "Gimme!" she begged. "I want to see what
I'm wearing."

I blocked her hand with my elbow. "It's just
the outfits for the party scene," I reminded her.

Luisa tried to snatch the envelope with her
other hand. "Then I want to see Jade's," she said.
"Don't you, Jade?" She glanced at my sister for sup-
port, but Jade had already put her earbuds into her
ears and was fiddling with her MP3 player.

I retreated a couple of yards away from Luisa.
"I think Mr. Kosloff wanted only *me* to see them,"
I said.

"You're no fun," Luisa sniffed.

As I stowed the envelope safely inside my bag,
I instantly felt better about *The Nutcracker*. Even if my
worst nightmare came true and my sloppy pirouettes
got me booted from the show, I was helping with the
costumes. At least I'd still feel like part of the show.

Before we'd gotten on the bus, Jade had called ahead to a pizzeria. Mom had given us money to get pizza for supper, and by the time we got off the bus on M Street, it was ready to pick up.

During the bus ride and on the walk home, I kept waiting for Jade to ask me how my rehearsal had gone today, so I could bring up my problem. But she looked so lost in her own world that I didn't say a word. *Was she still worrying about her own performance?* I wondered. After all, I was in just one of the numbers while she was in practically every scene. If you compared our visualization routines, mine was a three-minute cartoon while hers was an epic movie.

The smell of the pizza wafting up from the box was driving me crazy, and by the time Jade unlocked the front door, I was ready to tear open the box. The door had barely closed when we heard the patter of paws and our kitten, Tutu, came scurrying along the hall rug.

She looked ready to pounce on the pizza, too, so I shrugged off my dance bag and then lifted the box high over my head. "Tutu must smell the pepperoni," I said to Jade. "I think we'd better feed her first."

It was my fault, I guess. I'd made the mistake of slipping Tutu some pepperoni from my pizza a couple of times. Now, as a family member, she always demanded her fair share of it.

Jade nodded for me to go into the kitchen. "I'll make our salad. You take care of her," she said.

"Pizza's enough for me," I said.

"Mom gave me orders to make a salad," Jade said firmly. While she got some stuff from the fridge, I opened a tin of cat food. Usually, Tutu rubbed herself against anyone near the can opener, but today she was all eyes for the pizza. Just as I was dumping the cat food into her dish, she jumped onto a chair and tried to open the box with her paw.

Setting the cat dish down, I shooed Tutu off the chair. "That's people food," I scolded. But I felt a little sorry for her.

Without turning around, my sister added, "And no sneaking any pepperoni to her either."

"*Me-owr,*" Tutu said, which I'm pretty sure was feline-ese for "spoilsport."

As Jade poured salad from a bag into a bowl on the counter, I washed my hands and then got out some plates, silverware, and glasses.

"Ready," Jade finally said, crossing the kitchen to put the salad and a bottle of dressing on the table. The salad was in a large bowl of dark wood with inlaid patterns of lighter wood. Mom had traded one of her fabric pieces with another artist for it.

Tutu leaped onto my lap as soon as I sat down. I gently pushed her off, but her paws had no sooner touched the floor than she had bounded back onto my lap again. We repeated that several times before she stalked out of the kitchen sullenly.

"Sorry," I called after her, inhaling a delicious whiff of pizza as I finally got to lift the lid of the box.

Jade tapped my wrist. "Salad first," she reminded me.

My sister heaped salad onto my plate. I stared at the green hill in front of me. "I don't need all that," I insisted.

"The pizza's lukewarm," Jade said. "You can eat the salad while we heat it up."

"I think there's still some carrot cake left over from my birthday," I suggested. I'd just had my tenth birthday last week. "Carrots are vegetables. Can't I have that instead?"

"I said *salad*," Jade declared regally.

I'd had enough. "Who made you queen of the world?" I demanded to know. Grabbing a slice of pizza from the box, I put it on my plate.

Jade hesitated, but when I began eating and

making happy noises, she took a slice and began to eat as well. As we chewed, she indicated a spot on my right cheek where some sauce had splashed. I pointed to her left cheek, where she had a similar spot.

Grabbing a napkin, she leaned forward and began to clean my face. So I snatched up another napkin and returned the favor.

We were both laughing when we heard the *bump-bump-bump* of Mom's large wheeled suitcase outside the front door. The next moment there was a draft as the door opened and Mom came in, wheeling the bag behind her.

"How was the craft fair?" I asked.

Mom leaned the suitcase against the wall, crossed the room, and lifted the lid of the pizza box. She studied the pizza and then picked a slice with a lot of toppings.

If I had to eat salad, so did Mom. I slid my heaping plate of salad over to her. "Salad first," I said. Then I added just a little bit of salad to my plate, not the Mount Everest of greenery that Jade had given me.

Mom hesitated and gave the salad a sideways glance. "Why, thank you, Isabelle," she said. But she started with her pizza just as I had. Then she wiped her mouth and added, "The fair wasn't bad. I sold three pieces—the most expensive ones." She raised her eyebrows and grinned as she took another bite of pizza.

I held up what remained of my pizza in a kind of toast and said, "Congratulations."

"Thanks," said Mom and then asked, "How did the rehearsal go?"

"Um, I'm still learning the steps," I said carefully. Mom wasn't a dancer, so if I'd told her about my pirouette problem, all she could have done was given me a pep talk. *But maybe this is my chance to ask Jade for help*, I thought, stealing a glance at my sister.

Jade, though, hadn't heard a word I'd said. She sat lost in thought, her shoulders hunched over her dinner.

So I kept talking. "Mr. Kosloff saw my costume at the Autumn Festival and asked me to look at some of *The Nutcracker* costumes," I announced to Mom.

"Did he really?" she said, clearly impressed. "Well, he's a smart man. I'm proud of you, honey."

Mom took a bite of salad and then glanced at Jade. "And how are things going for you?" she asked, nudging Jade's shoulder.

My sister shrugged. "Fine," she said.

Before Mom could press for more, Dad came

home. "Pizza?" he called from the hallway. "Just what the doctor ordered."

"What're you doing back so early?" Mom called.

"We drove through all that traffic over to Silver Springs," Dad complained as he strode into the kitchen, "but when we got to the restaurant, we found out that the company had canceled the party. Nobody thought about calling us."

I put some pizza slices onto a plate for him. "They ought to pay you anyway," I said.

"That's what I'm going to argue, but we'll see. The company I was supposed to play for is a law firm, after all," Dad said as he sat down. "But let's forget about gigs. I think this is the first time we've gotten to eat together in a while."

Jade was heaping salad into a bowl for him. "Do we need name tags?" she asked, grinning.

Mom stared at all the skin exposed on my sister's forearms. "Jade, you really must be growing," she said. "Look at those sleeves!"

Jade hid her arms under the table as she sat back down. "Actually," she mumbled, "I think this sweater just shrank in the dryer. I guess I didn't read the label before I threw it in. Sorry."

Mom frowned. "I appreciate that you're helping with the laundry during the holidays, Jade," she said, "but we talked about being careful. That sweater was expensive."

"I said I was sorry," Jade said as she began to eat sullenly.

"No harm done," Dad said, trying to smooth things over in his usual way—with a joke. "Wash it a couple more times and Tutu can wear it instead."

"Why are you both picking on me?" Jade asked sharply. I thought I saw tears at the corners of her eyes. "First Mom. Now you, Dad. Why can't you just leave me alone?"

"Take it easy, Jade," said Dad, puzzled. "What's gotten into you?"

Jade's chair scraped the kitchen linoleum as she stood up. "You wouldn't understand," she snapped. Sliding her still-full plate onto the counter, she left the kitchen.

Mom sighed. "So much for a nice family dinner together," she said.

We all listened to Jade stomp angrily up the steps. The next moment I heard our bedroom door slam.

Dad scratched his head, puzzled. "Did some

aliens steal our Jade and leave an angry clone behind?" he asked.

"She's just worried about the show," I said. "After all, she's got a big part."

Dad glanced at Mom. "Should we go upstairs and talk to her about it?" he asked.

Just then, we heard the dance music begin to play from Act One of *The Nutcracker*. Mom listened for a moment and then shook her head. "Let's give her some time," she said. "You know what a perfectionist Jade is. She's got a lot riding on her shoulders. She'll be okay once the show starts."

But this was my sister's favorite music. She couldn't just sit and listen to it. We should be hearing the *thump* of her feet as she danced.

Something was really bothering her, and I was going to find out what.

CHAPTER 5

Clara's Costume

I carried our dance bags up to the room that I shared with Jade, but when I opened the door, everything was dark. I flipped on the light switch. My sister was sitting on her bed with her knees drawn up and her chin resting on top of them.

"Go away," she mumbled.

"It's my room, too," I said. I unslung the bags from my shoulders and dumped them on the floor. Tutu had followed me into our room, and she circled our bags, sniffing for traces of pepperoni, as I started to change into my pajamas.

Jade hid her face against her knees. "Are Mom and Dad mad at me?" she asked in a muffled voice.

I shook my head. "Mom and Dad know how much pressure you're under," I said.

Jade lifted her head and said angrily, "I can do Clara, you know."

I'd never seen Jade like this. My sister was an amazing dancer. There was nothing she couldn't do, and she had always acted like she knew it. So what was upsetting her now?

"I know you can," I assured Jade. "Has Mr. Kosloff been giving you a hard time?"

Jade shook her head and buried her face again.

It wasn't easy trying to find the right next question. I felt as if I was tiptoeing around.

"What are the other dancers like?" I asked. I wondered if any of them were bugging Jade the way Renata bugged me.

"Why are you asking so many questions?" she snapped.

As the music began to replay on her laptop, the notes swirled around us, filling the awkward silence.

"If you want to practice, I'll go back downstairs," I finally offered.

"No, do what you want," Jade mumbled.

Up until now, Jade had practiced every chance she got. Something was really wrong, but I couldn't figure out what. Maybe the best I could do was to take her mind off her problems for a little while. It seemed strange, though, to be the one trying to help her. She was the one who was always coming to *my* rescue.

"Want to see your outfit then?" I asked. Unzipping my bag, I took out the big brown envelope with the sketches. Tutu immediately dove inside the bag, and the sides of the bag twitched as she poked about.

Jade hesitated. "You told Luisa that you were the only one who could look at them," she said.

"Well, Luisa might be my best friend, but

she's lousy at keeping secrets," I said. "But, hey, if you really don't want to look . . ."

Jade smiled weakly. "You know I do," she said.

I stuck my hands into my bag and retrieved Tutu. A towel had gotten snagged on her claws, and I eased it off. Then I opened the envelope of sketches.

Looking at these designs, I felt as if it were already Christmas. Besides a few people at HDC, we were the first ones to see the party costumes. Jade sat up straight as I excitedly flipped through the sketches.

When I saw the costumes for the mice and the soldiers, I realized that Margie must have misunderstood Mr. Kosloff and given me *all* the kids' costumes for Act One instead of just the party outfits. I slid the battle costumes back into the envelope and began to go through the party designs. Mr. Kosloff had made a lot of notes and cross-outs on each page. When I saw Clara's outfit, I held it up dramatically. "Ta-da!" I announced.

Jade stood up so that she could look at the outfit more closely. It had a fitted lavender top with long sleeves and a skirt with a sheer layer over a full flaring underlayer. We studied the design. "It's pretty," I said, "but . . . it could be better."

Mr. Kosloff had scribbled notes in the margin

37

beside Jade's party dress. Jade jabbed her finger at one of the notes. "Lavender isn't my color," she said. "I should be wearing light blue. And look at how long those sleeves are. They make this look like an old lady's dress."

"Light blue is fine up close," I said. "But on the stage in a big theater, you have to have a color that will make you stand out." I studied her complexion. "It should be red."

"I want light blue," she said.

I shook my head firmly. "Red."

"You asked for my opinion," Jade argued.

"No, I asked you if you wanted to look at the designs," I countered. "It was just to satisfy your curiosity."

"I know what color's best for me," she snapped as she flopped back down on her bed.

Mr. Kosloff wanted my opinion, not yours, is what I thought to myself, but I just said, "You're right about the sleeves." I thought about shortening them, but that didn't seem to be enough. So I drew the dress without sleeves. "How's this?" I asked, showing her my revisions.

Jade picked up her earbuds and fiddled with the cord. "Better," was all she said.

I thought that after making such a fuss about the dress, Jade might be more excited about the new sketch. So I looked at it again. Something still seemed off. "Do you think the dress is too plain?" I asked. "After all, you're the star of the party."

"Just do what you want," she said. "You're not going to listen to me anyway."

I tried to control my temper. "*Jade*," I said, "what's bugging you?"

She shook her head and looked away. "Don't worry about it, Isabelle," she said. "Mr. Kosloff made some changes to my routine that I've got to remember." She plugged her earbuds into her laptop and then fitted them snugly into her ears. Closing her eyes, she began to listen to the music again. She must have been visualizing her routine, because every now and then she'd move her arm or her wrist.

Jade couldn't fool me. Whatever was bothering my sister was more than just a few changes to her routine. I had to find out what it was—and try to help her fix it.

I carried the envelope of costume designs downstairs, planning to look at them in the living room. But I bumped into Mom as she was coming out of her sewing room.

"Just the girl I wanted to see," she said. Pulling me inside, she led me over to a tall white armoire against the far wall of the room. When she opened the doors of the armoire, I stared in amazement. Usually the shelves of the armoire were crammed with fabric and piles of stuff from Mom's work, like photos and X-rays of old dresses from the Smithsonian. But today the shelves were clean and bare, except for a white wicker sewing basket, a tidy pile of colorful fabric swatches, and the small purple sewing machine that Mom sometimes let me use. She lifted the sewing basket off the shelf and showed me what was inside: spools of thread, a tape measure, a pair of scissors, and a pincushion.

"For you," Mom announced, waving her hand toward the armoire with a flourish. "I thought you could make this your own and work on your designs in here."

I knew that space was precious in a room filled with stuff from floor to ceiling. "Mom, really?" I said.

She gave me a little hug. "I know you want to be a dancer, Isabelle," she said, "but I think you've got a talent for design, too. I'd like you to keep developing that when you can." She pointed me toward the oak desk that had belonged to my grandfather. "I cleared off some space at my desk for you, too," she added.

As I sat down in the chair in front of the desk, I felt like a queen in her castle.

"You'll find colored pencils and erasers in the drawer," Mom said. "Is there anything else you need?"

I shook my head, almost too happy to speak. When I set the envelope on the desk, Mom started to reach for it but pulled her hand back.

"Do you want to see the designs?" I asked.

Mom looked tempted, but then she shook her head. "If I look at them, I'll wind up making comments," she said. "And Mr. Kosloff wanted your ideas, not mine." She bit her lip, as if holding back something else.

"Spill," I said. "I can see you want to tell me something."

Mom nodded and smiled. "Just remember one thing," she said. "An outfit not only has to look good on paper, but it also has to look and move well when a real person wears it."

I thought about some of the clothes I had drawn when I was small. "Like a dress that looks slim and neat on paper but would be so tight, you could hardly walk in it?" I asked.

"That's it," Mom said. "Don't stay up too late, Isabelle, okay?" She kissed my forehead and left to get ready for bed.

I kept Mom's advice in mind as I began to go through the party outfits. Though all of the costumes looked danceable, I had suggestions for how to improve most of them—I couldn't help it! Sometimes all I did was suggest a new color or pattern. Other times I widened a collar or lengthened a cuff or suggested a thinner belt. The ideas just kept coming.

After I had written my notes and drawn my sketches by the designs for the party outfits, I should have stopped there. But I couldn't help sneaking a peek at the other designs from the battle scene. The soldiers' uniforms were colorful enough, but the mice looked like weasels to me.

Since I wasn't supposed to have seen those designs, I should have just slipped them back into the envelope with the other stuff. But they bothered me. Why would weasels invade a house? I know the mice were supposed to be the villains, but these designs seemed too scary. Mice should look like mice, so I wrote a suggestion that the muzzles be shorter and rounder. I wasn't sure Mr. Kosloff would understand my note, so I made a sketch, too.

Then I almost erased it, afraid that Mr. Kosloff would get mad at me for doing more than I was supposed to. And had I gone too far in the other direction and made the mice too cute? I got as far as touching the eraser to the paper, but I didn't use it. When something felt not quite right, I had to do something about it. So I slid the mouse sketch into the envelope with everything else.

Jade was already asleep when I crept upstairs and into our room. Tutu was curled up next to her. As I crawled into my own bed, I glanced at my sister. Helping Mr. Kosloff had been easy. Helping Jade was going to be a lot harder. But I wasn't going to give up.

CHAPTER 6

The Partygoers

I was trapped inside a huge clear plastic ball. Giant weasels were chasing me. As I ran, my ball rolled forward. But the weasels were gaining on me. One of them reached out a paw.

When I felt the touch on my shoulder, I sat up with a shout.

Jade jumped back from my bed. "Yikes!" she squealed. "You scared me."

"Ditto," I said, trying to catch my breath. "I was having a nightmare."

"Then it's a good thing that I woke you up," Jade said. "Come on. We have to get to the theater. We're all rehearsing together today."

As far as I was concerned, I'd just swapped one nightmare for another. Mr. Kosloff was going to go through all the children's scenes today because he wanted to see how we were doing. So this would be his first chance to see Isabelle the Human Bowling Ball in action.

Ms. Ferri had been nice yesterday, but how long would Mr. Kosloff put up with my pirouettes before he'd ask Renata to take my place? I was sure she expected that. Wherever she was right now, she was probably grinning ear to ear.

I put on a sequined purple leotard and purple

jazz pants and went downstairs with Jade. My sister had made a point of wearing a light blue top and skirt over pale green leggings and light blue leg warmers.

Mom had already left for another craft fair in Virginia, but Dad's wedding gig wasn't until later that afternoon. Normally Dad liked to sleep late on weekends, so I was surprised to see him already up. "How are my two favorite daughters?" he asked, trying to sound cheerful. "I thought I'd make breakfast for you."

I think the meal was his way of trying to make up with Jade after last night's fight.

"That'd be real nice," I said.

"Ta-da!" Dad announced, proudly holding up two packets of instant oatmeal. Ripping them open, he dumped the contents into bowls and added water from a steaming kettle. "This'll stick to your ribs."

"It smells good," I said, using a spoon to stir one of the bowls.

Dad held up his hand. "Wait, wait, this is a high-class joint, you know," he said. He peeled a banana, sliced it up, and heaped so many pieces into each bowl that the oatmeal disappeared.

As we ate, Dad tried to chat with us, and

though I answered him, Jade merely grunted. When we were finished, she finally spoke one word: "Thanks."

I put our bowls in the sink and stood on tiptoe to kiss Dad. "Yeah, thanks, Dad," I told him.

It was a little chilly as Jade and I walked to the bus stop, so I slid my hands into the pockets of my heavy jacket. Though Jade was right next to me, she was lost in her own little world. Her earbuds were snug in her ears. Was she visualizing her routine *again*? I probably should have been doing the same thing, but I was too busy checking the buses. Somebody had to make sure we got on the right one and wound up at the HDC rather than in Maryland.

We took the bus as far as Dupont Circle, where we got off and walked toward the tall steel-and-concrete HDC theater and offices.

A small girl turned to watch as we entered the stage door on the side. When I was little and my parents had taken me to a ballet program, I'd been just as curious about the dancers I saw going backstage. I felt a tiny thrill. Did this little girl wish she were me?

Just inside the door, a guard sat on a folding chair near a giant photo of Anna Hart, the founder

of the HDC—as well as the performing arts school
I attended. Fingerprints smudged the glass because
dancers liked to touch it for good luck. Jade touched
the framed photo gently, and so did I.

The guard buzzed us through a second door,
and we entered the part of the theater that the public
never saw. The walls here were plain cinder blocks
painted white, and pipes and conduits ran along the
ceiling. We could have been inside a factory instead
of a theater. It was such a contrast from the lobby,
like the difference between stagehands in sweatshirts
backstage and ballerinas in pretty costumes beneath
the spotlight.

When we got to the second floor, the doors to
Studio A hadn't opened yet, so the corridors were
filled with kids. Luisa waved her hand, and we
squeezed through the crowd toward her.

"It's like a rush-hour traffic jam," she said to us.

"What's the holdup?" I asked.

"They say Mr. Kosloff's working out some
changes in the choreography," Luisa said.

When kids began to swivel around and point,
I turned and saw the company members making their
way toward us. Until now, it had just been young
dancers like us practicing their routines on weekends

while the professional dancers rehearsed during the week. Today, though, Jade and the partygoers would dance with the professionals for the first time.

Since I'd seen these dancers only in costumes onstage, it was strange to see them in regular clothes. It was even stranger to see them with paper cups of coffee or tea in their hands. The dancers were standing just a few feet away from us now, but it might as well have been a mile. I felt tongue-tied, and I saw that my friends and castmates were staring at the professional dancers with wide eyes, too.

I felt Jade reach for my hand. *The Nutcracker* sounded faint and tinny from her dangling earbuds. "I'm sorry about last night," she said softly. "I'm really glad you're here with me."

I thought about my bowling-ball routine to come and said, "I'm glad you're here, too."

About ten minutes later, Bettina, the blonde artistic associate I had seen teaching the little mice yesterday, let us inside Studio A. It was the HDC's largest studio. As we stepped through the doorway, Luisa gasped. "Oh, wow," she said, and I followed her gaze inside. Mr. Kosloff was standing in the center of the floor, and just beside him was our idol, Jackie Sanchez. I felt a flutter of excitement in my chest.

The Partygoers

Jackie had studied at Anna Hart and become a principal dancer at New York City Ballet. I'd seen her from about forty feet away when she'd come to our Autumn Festival. Now she was only ten feet away and was wearing capris and a sweater instead of the costume she wore on festival night.

I'd heard a rumor that Jackie Sanchez was in D.C. and was coaching some of the HDC dancers, but I hadn't expected her to be here today. It was amazing to see her again in person, yet as I watched her demonstrate a few arm movements for one of the company members, I felt my excitement slowly turn to dread. If I couldn't pull off my pirouettes today, I would not only embarrass myself in front of the cast and Mr. Kosloff, but I would humiliate myself in front of my *idol*, too.

To make matters worse, I caught Renata's eye as we pushed through the now-crowded studio. She smirked and whispered something to Emilio. I strained my ears, but I couldn't hear what she said— though I was pretty sure it was about me.

When Jade, Luisa, and I found an empty space, we set our bags down and began to stretch and warm up with the rest of the cast. Mr. Kosloff and Jackie Sanchez took their seats to observe the dancers, and

Bettina pulled up a chair next to them, occasionally calling out greetings to the dancers who would play her mice. Then Mr. Kosloff clapped his hands loudly and announced, "Attention, everyone. We're going to take it from the top."

The dancers who would play the partygoers stepped to the center of the room with their props—cell phones, handheld games, and tablets. As they danced, they busily interacted with their devices but hardly looked at one another. I watched the party scene play out, thinking about the envelope of costume designs tucked in my dance bag. Except for Clara, I knew that the other kids would be wearing drab colors like grays, browns, and dark blues. I think the idea was to show how boring their world was.

I'd spent most of the time last night working on the girls' dresses, but now I pictured the boys' costumes in my mind. In Mr. Kosloff's designs, the boys were all wearing dress pants with long-sleeved sweaters or blazers. But suddenly those designs seemed too formal to me. *Shouldn't some of the boys be in button-down shirts or even T-shirts?* I wondered.

I snuck the envelope out of my bag and scrunched down low so that I could make a quick note on a boy's costume sketch.

The party scene picked up when the dancer playing Drosselmeyer the Toymaker arrived. He immediately got disgusted when he saw everyone ignoring one another. With a wave of his hand, all of their electronic devices went dead.

He quieted the protests by entertaining the partygoers with his magical dolls, which were actually played by adult dancers who moved their arms and legs stiffly, in a doll-like way. As I watched them dance, I wondered what costumes they would be wearing. If I were the designer, I would put the dolls in the brightest costumes possible so that they would stand out from the partygoers.

After the last doll performed, the partygoers finally began to dance and talk with one another. Drosselmeyer danced with my sister and then presented the Nutcracker to her. Cradling her gift, Jade seemed to glide above the stage as if dancing on air. I thought of how the flared skirt of her costume would twirl around her as she moved. Yet something still felt plain about it—too blah for Jade's amazing dancing. The dress needed more than color to stand out and be worthy of the dancer wearing it. But what?

After the party scene, Bettina's little mice arrived, and all thoughts of costumes flew out of my mind. Though the little dancers were wearing regular practice outfits today, I recognized Addison and the other two wandering mice from yesterday.

As the mice began to dance about the studio, they wagged their heads from side to side and swaggered, just as I had told them to do. They were mice with attitude. Addison even waved at me as she danced by. I felt a little proud that Mr. Kosloff had kept my suggestions for their routine.

When Jade came to get the Nutcracker she'd left behind, the mice began to play pranks on her. That's when the Nutcracker came to life—played by a boy named Paul Sommers in a mask. The Nutcracker led the toy soldiers in defending Jade.

The battle went back and forth, but just when it seemed as if the mice were going to win, Jade threw her slipper at the Mouse King. She had practiced pitching shoes at home, so her aim was dead center. That distracted the Mouse King, and the Nutcracker was able to kill him. But the Mouse King managed to stab the Nutcracker, too, before he died.

As the mice and soldiers withdrew, Jade wept over the dying Nutcracker. But then Drosselmeyer the Toymaker appeared, and with magical passes of his hands, he healed the Nutcracker. When Paul sat up, he took off his mask to reveal a prince with brown hair.

Jade rose and did a little dance, first of surprise and then of joy. She was as lovely as ever, every position perfect.

And then Paul stood up.

"I wonder how she likes looking at the top of his head?" I heard someone say from a cluster of dancers in the corner. I turned and saw a girl with a ponytail giggling with a boy wearing glasses standing next to her.

Looking back at the dance floor, I noticed for the first time that Paul was a couple of inches shorter than Jade.

It sounded to me as if someone was jealous of my sister. I shot an angry glance at the girl.

As Jade and the prince continued their dance, though, the boy with glasses snickered. "Paul, do you need a ladder?" he said, just loud enough for Jade and Paul to hear.

I instantly saw Jade's reaction. Her shoulders hunched, as if she was trying to make herself appear smaller. With each step now, her legs and arms began to move unsteadily. *Is this what has been bothering my sister? I wondered. Her height?*

I saw Paul's lips move. I'm pretty sure he was

whispering to my sister to ignore the gigglers. But when one of them laughed again out loud, Jade stumbled. "I'm sorry," she blurted out.

"Keep going," Mr. Kosloff called from the other side of the room. "We've nearly finished Act One."

So Jade kept on dancing, but she seemed stiff and awkward now. I was stunned. I'd never seen her dance this badly before. I might mess up a performance now and then, but my perfect sister never did.

As the piano played the last note, Jade stood still, looking like a prisoner waiting to be shot.

"Let's take a break, everyone," Mr. Kosloff announced. "I'll give you all your notes after we finish the Mother Ginger scene."

Jade immediately headed for the door, picking up her pace until she was running.

CHAPTER 7

Sisters in Waiting

I ran after Jade, but by the time I reached the doorway, it was crowded with other dancers trying to get out. I managed to squeeze into the hallway. When I didn't spot Jade, I went into the women's restroom and found her crying in front of the sink.

A couple of girls whispered to each other as they left the restroom. I went over and stood by Jade, rubbing her back silently because I didn't know what to say.

"I knew this would happen," Jade sobbed. "Mr. Kosloff's going to drop me because I'm too tall."

So that *was* what had been bothering her.

"If Mr. Kosloff was going to replace you, he would have done it by now," I reasoned. "He must really want you as his Clara."

Jade squeezed her eyes shut and moaned, "But I was so, *so* awful."

I got some paper towels and wet them under a faucet. "I know what a good dancer you are," I said soothingly. "So does Mr. Kosloff."

Jade shook her head. "I can't go back into that studio," she said.

"But you can't quit dancing either," I insisted as I held the damp towels out to her.

Jade wiped her face. She blew her nose and

then said, "At least I'll get to see *you* dance."

When Jade mentioned my own dance routine, I felt as if she'd just dropped an ice cube down my back. I'd been so busy thinking about costumes—and then worrying about Jade—that I'd forgotten my own problems. I hadn't even taken the time to visualize my routine, not that I was sure it would have done any good. But I couldn't freak out now. I had to follow my own advice to Jade and march back into that studio.

When we entered the studio, Ms. Ferri waved her hand and said, "Come to Mama Ginger, Isabelle." Tape had been placed on the floor to approximate the stage, and my stomach did flip-flops as I followed Ms. Ferri over to a place stage right.

"Try not to knock us all over, Bowling-Ball Belle," Renata whispered to me as I lined up next to her.

That didn't help my nerves any, but Luisa leaped to my defense. "You worry about yourself, Renata," she snapped.

Renata glared at her but said nothing.

As we gathered around Ms. Ferri, my eyes searched for Jade. I found her leaning against the wall in the far corner of the studio. She still looked miserable. Even though she had said she wanted to see me dance, she couldn't seem to shake the memory of her own mistakes. That scared me. If a great dancer like Jade had started to doubt herself, what chance did I have?

"Okay, crouch," Ms. Ferri said.

I was in the front row, with Renata on my right and Luisa on my left. We all leaned forward with our hands on our knees.

All the other dancers were watching us. Even the company members had stayed. We'd never had an audience before.

As the music started, Ms. Ferri began to stamp her feet. On the fifth count, she took a step to the side. When she brought her feet together again, I moved my foot to the side with the rest of the cast.

Step.

Step.

Step.

Stride by stride, we moved slowly across the floor. Something felt off, though. Then I realized we had a different pianist today: a man named Phil, who provided the music for the party rehearsals. Though the score was the same, he played some of the notes a little differently than Claude did.

Everyone managed to adjust so that we didn't bump into one another. But I breathed a sigh of relief when Ms. Ferri finally found her place and stopped.

"Up goes the flap," she murmured.

Still crouching, I took two steps away from her, but I was so afraid of making a mistake that I was a little stiff. I did more of a series of hops than real leaps.

"Smile, Isabelle," Ms. Ferri whispered. "Remember: July Fourth, Christmas, Arbor Day."

I pulled up the corners of my mouth, but I don't think I fooled anyone.

As I neared Emilio, I imagined the toy top in my mind and got ready to spin. It worked! I pirouetted away from his hands. Everything went smoothly with Agnes, too.

As I neared Renata, though, she whispered. "Mr. Kosloff's watching. Don't screw this up."

I didn't need her to tell me that. *You are a top, you are a top,* I told myself, trying to block out Renata's words. *Spin, spin, spin.*

But all of my muscles were tense now, and even as I started my pirouette, I could feel myself losing my balance.

"Watch out!" Renata protested as I rammed into her, and we both fell to the floor.

I heard the audience gasp, and Ms. Ferri quickly asked, "Are you okay, girls?"

I nodded as I bounced to my feet. I couldn't even look at Renata—I didn't want to see the expression on her face.

As I moved on, I heard a boy in the audience say, "I thought this was a ballet, not a wrestling match."

"Best two falls out of three?" another boy called.

By the time I reached Luisa, I just wanted to hide in the restroom and cry like my sister. I managed to pull off some sort of pirouette, and then returned to Ms. Ferri and crouched low, my cheeks burning. I felt Ms. Ferri squeeze my shoulder encouragingly as we lurched offstage.

All I wanted to do was get back to Jade. Right now, she was the only one who would understand how I felt. Tears stung the corners of my eyes as Luisa and I wove our way through the crowd of dancers and made our way over to my sister.

As I passed by Jackie Sanchez, I looked away. I didn't want to see what she thought of me.

Jade was sitting down cross-legged now. As I dropped down beside her, she took my hand sympathetically. Luisa sat down on my other side, nudging my shoulder with hers.

We sat there, listening as Mr. Kosloff gave his notes to the other dancers. Jade and I tightened our grip, waiting for our turn, but it never came. I guessed that Mr. Kosloff didn't want to waste his time. Why bother if he was going to dump us?

But as rehearsal started to break up, Mr. Kosloff called us over to him. My stomach did full-on somersaults as I rose to my feet.

"Good luck," Luisa whispered, giving me an anxious look.

"Thanks," I said. "We're going to need it."

As the others streamed out of the studio, Jade and I walked over to Mr. Kosloff, who was standing with Jackie Sanchez. I still couldn't look at her.

Mr. Kosloff ran a hand over his head. "What happened, Jade, Isabelle?" he asked.

Neither Jade nor I knew where to begin, so we kept quiet. I stared at my feet, waiting for the axe to fall. But I couldn't help sneaking a sideways peek at Jade. In my wildest nightmares, I had never thought *anyone* would be disappointed with her dancing.

"You've been fine in rehearsals, Jade, so
I know you've managed to adjust for your growth
spurt," Mr. Kosloff said. "But things are going to happen onstage and off and with the audience. You can't
let it get to you." He gave a chuckle. "Once, during a
show, the elastic on my tights broke. So I had to dance
with one hand holding them up."

I giggled in spite of myself and looked up at
Mr. Kosloff. I even stole a glance at Jackie Sanchez,
who gave me a warm, encouraging smile.

Mr. Kosloff tapped a fingertip against his forehead. "The point is to stay focused, Jade, okay?" he
said.

Jade blinked. "You're not dropping me?" she
asked in a small voice.

Mr. Kosloff looked surprised. "No, of course
not," he said. "When you auditioned, you were so
graceful that I said 'Wow!' I know you can make our
audiences say the same thing."

I saw my sister relax beside me. Then it was
my turn for Mr. Kosloff's notes. "And when I saw you
the first time, Isabelle, your leaps were so strong and
powerful. You were a regular dynamo. Today, though,
you let your mistakes get to you."

I let Renata get to me, too, I thought.

Mr. Kosloff went on. "You just hopped around like a tired little frog. As for your pirouettes, well"—he shrugged—"they were fine during the audition. So I'd say go back to basics. Really practice them at home."

"Yes, sir. Thank you," I said gratefully.

And then Jackie spoke up. "And don't be afraid to make mistakes, Isabelle."

I felt another shot of anxiety. My idol was speaking directly to me, and I couldn't process her words. Was she encouraging me to make mistakes?

"Dancers are human beings, not machines," Jackie went on. "We all make errors. So instead of focusing on perfection, try to focus on the *joy* of dance. Dancing is supposed to be fun, right?"

I nodded. Dancing had always been fun for me. I remembered how it had been when I was very little. Mom had said I never stopped dancing around the house. My parents had to put everything breakable out of reach of my hands and feet.

"So when something goes wrong onstage, you've got to have a short memory," Jackie said firmly. "Shake it off and keep going. Concentrate on having fun. You can do that, can't you?"

Jackie paused then, waiting for my response.

I had never expected to get this close to my idol—let alone have her give me advice. I opened my mouth, but all that came out was, "Uh . . ."

Say something, I told myself. *Say anything.* But the words had drained out of my brain. All I could do was nod again.

Clasping his hands behind him, Mr. Kosloff leaned toward me. "Now I think it's your turn to give *me* notes, Isabelle," he said.

Huh? Then it hit me: the costume sketches. "Yes, sir," I said quickly. Feeling as if I were dreaming, I pulled the envelope from my bag and handed it to Mr. Kosloff.

As he took it, Mr. Kosloff smiled. "You weren't too brutal on these designs, were you?" he asked.

Jade spoke up from beside me. "My sister will definitely tell you what she thinks," she said, grinning at me. And then she added, "But when it comes to fashion, she does know what's good."

I shot Jade a grateful glance. She and I might argue at home, but she was always ready to stick up for me around other people.

Mr. Kosloff pretended to shiver. "I can't wait for the verdict," he joked.

"Excuse me, Mr. Kosloff," Bettina interrupted,

tapping her watch. "The next cast will be coming in for their rehearsals in a half hour, and we have things to discuss."

Mr. Kosloff clutched the envelope. "I'm sorry, Isabelle. There's no time to talk," he said. "But did you write your comments on the designs?"

"Yes, sir," I said. "And there are pictures, too," I added nervously, wondering again if I had gone too far in my critique.

Mr. Kosloff saluted me with the envelope. "Excellent!" he said. "Thank you, Isabelle."

I smiled and started to turn away, but Jackie wasn't finished with me yet. "You seem to be a girl of many talents," she said to me.

First, advice from Jackie Sanchez—and now compliments. I felt as if fireworks were going off inside my head. I fought the urge to break into a happy dance, and from the joyful bounce in my sister's step as she led me back toward the hallway, I could tell she felt the same way.

When we got home, Dad had already left for his wedding gig, but Mom had made lasagna and left it in the fridge, along with a salad. As Jade pulled out the pan of lasagna, she asked, "When did you start having problems with your pirouettes?"

I cracked open a can of cat food for Tutu. "I've been having trouble since rehearsals started," I admitted.

Jade cut two squares of lasagna, put them on a large plate, and slid it into the microwave. "Why didn't you tell me?" she asked as she turned around and leaned against the counter.

I shrugged. I scooped the cat food into a bowl and set it in front of Tutu. "You've been sort of touchy lately," I said, without meeting Jade's eyes. "Why didn't you tell me what was bugging *you*?"

Jade's face fell. She turned to pull silverware out of a drawer. "There wasn't anything you could do about it, Isabelle," she said.

I wanted to argue with that, but I couldn't. Jade's height was definitely out of my control.

My mouth began to water at the aroma coming from the microwave. Mom's lasagna smelled delicious, as usual.

Jade and I ate our dinner silently. It wasn't until we were nearly full that Jade spoke again. "Just how are you visualizing your routine?" she asked.

She was sounding a lot more like the big sister

I remembered—the one who would drop everything to help me. I guess she was feeling a little better now that she knew Mr. Kosloff wasn't going to drop her from her big role in *The Nutcracker.*

When I told Jade how I visualized the steps in my routine as toys in a toy chest, she pursed her lips. "Well, that all sounds good," she said. "So maybe we just need to go back to basics like Mr. Kosloff said. We'll concentrate on your pirouettes." She glanced at the clock. "But we'd better wait until tomorrow. I've got science homework to do tonight."

I was ready to crawl into bed and fall asleep myself, but it was time to change from ballerina into student. "And I've got to study for a math quiz," I confessed.

I guess solving our other problems was just going to have to wait.

CHAPTER 8

A Magic Trick

On Monday, I had trouble maneuvering through the crowd in the hallway at school. Luisa was leaning against a row of lockers when I joined her. "You got here just in time to watch. Some kids talked Gabe into doing a magic trick," she whispered, nodding toward our friend, who was on the other side of the corridor.

"Is this your card?" Gabriel was asking a red-headed girl. He fanned out a deck of cards. Only the queen of hearts was faceup among them.

"Yes, that's it," the girl gasped.

When Gabriel saw me, he gave me a warm smile. He flipped the queen over and tucked it back into the deck. "Well, thanks everybody," he said. "But I've got to be going."

"Do another trick," a boy urged. "I'll choose this time."

Gabriel surprised me when he didn't do more. Instead he held up his hands. "Sorry, folks," he said. "That's it for today."

He joined Luisa and me as the disappointed crowd started to break up. "Luisa told me about yesterday," he said. "You okay?" He looked concerned.

"Yeah, if you're not in the show," Luisa declared, "then I'm not either. I'll quit."

Good old Luisa. I didn't know many dancers—
or friends—who would make that kind of sacrifice.
"Thanks," I said, "but everything's fine. Mr. Kosloff
just told Jade and me not to let things distract us."
I added with a grin, "So did Jackie Sanchez."

Gabriel let out a whistle. "Jackie Sanchez spoke
to you?" he said.

I motioned to the distance between us. "I was
this close to her," I bragged.

Luisa smiled wickedly. "Just wait until I tell
Renata," she said.

"Don't do that," I said. "She's already so
pumped full of jealousy that she might explode."

Luisa's eyebrows twitched. "That's the idea,"
she joked.

With a grin, I turned to Gabriel. "So just how
do you do that card trick?" I asked.

Gabriel let out a mock sigh. "I keep telling
you," he said. "A true magician never reveals his
secrets."

"And I'm going to keep asking until you spill,"
I prodded.

Gabriel hesitated. "If I tell you the secret for this
one trick," he said, "will you promise to stop bothering me and never share the secret with anyone else?"

"I swear," I said.

"Same here," Luisa said. We leaned in closer to our friend.

Gabriel fanned out the deck in his hands. "Pick a card," he instructed me.

I slid the four of diamonds out of the middle of the deck.

"As I ask you to show the card to everyone else," he said, "no one's watching me turn the deck over in my other hand." He nodded toward his left hand. "So those cards are all faceup." When he lifted the deck again, his hand was covering it, so I couldn't see that the cards were showing their fronts now. "Then, without letting me see the card, I ask you to put it back in."

Turning the four of diamonds over so that it was facedown, I eased it back into the deck.

"I ask you to concentrate on what the card is and maybe tell some jokes," Gabriel explained. "In the meantime, no one's noticed that I've lowered my hand with the deck and reversed it so that all the other cards are facedown again." He fanned out the cards so that only the four of diamonds was faceup. "But yours is there plain as day."

He stowed the deck away. "The real secret is

that I get people to see what I want them to see and not notice what I don't want them to," he said. "It's called 'misdirection.'"

"Misdirection," I repeated. "That's a great trick, Gabe."

In fact, I wish I could use that in dance, I thought as I followed my friends down the hall to our lockers. *Wouldn't it be great if I could misdirect the audience's eyes away from me every time I was about to do a pirouette?*

As soon as school was over, Jade and I headed straight home and went into the living room.

Jade crouched by the sofa. "Isabelle, help me shove back the couch," she ordered.

We wound up moving all the furniture against the walls to clear even more space. That set Mom's artwork, "Pond Dreams," twirling above us.

After a visit to a water lily pond at Kenilworth Park, Mom had fit different fabrics over wires and hung them from the ceiling. Together, they formed a water lily in bloom among green lily pads and rippling water. The slightest breeze set the parts in motion so that the mobile was constantly changing, just like the real pond.

A Magic Trick

The single water lily floating in the center caught my eye, as always. The V-shaped ripples on the pond surrounding the lily all seemed to point toward it. The dangling art caught Tutu's eyes, too, because she hopped onto the sofa and then sprang toward the mobile. As she fell short and the fabric shapes spun faster, an idea began teasing at the back of my brain. Before I could put my finger on it, Jade twirled her hand around and said, "Okay, make like a top, Isabelle."

As I took my position on our homemade stage, Jade sat cross-legged on the sofa. I stood up on my right leg and bent my left, beginning my pirouette. I started out strong, as usual, but slowly the room began to tilt around me as I lost my balance. I stumbled out of the turn but didn't fall.

"Again," Jade said. And again and again. After my sixth botched pirouette, Jade rose from the couch. "I think I see the problem," she announced.

I stood to the side, and Jade moved to the center of the floor. "You've been concentrating so much on your footwork that you forgot about your arms," she said. "You're holding them too far away from your sides. When you turn, centrifugal force pulls your arms out, and that throws you off balance." As Jade demonstrated a pirouette, she kept her arms far away from her ribs as she spun, and sure enough, she wobbled toward the end. "You've got to keep your arms in closer."

Raising her arms in perfect form, she tried the pirouette again and did it easily. "Now you try," she said, sitting back down on the couch.

I bent my arms and held them slightly away from my sides, trying to copy my sister. I squeezed my eyes shut for just a moment, imagining the spinning toy top. Then I opened my eyes and began. This time, when I spun, I did it without tilting.

Jade clapped her hands together. "You've got it!" she cheered.

I turned again and then again, just for the sheer joy of it. "Mr. Kosloff was right," I said happily. "It's back to basics."

Now I was more determined than ever to help Jade, too. "What can I do for you?" I asked her.

Jade shrugged, resigned. "Unless you can take a few inches off me," she said, "there's nothing."

I stood there, feeling bad for Jade, when a furry missile shot by me. Tutu's paws stretched for the water lily again, but she missed badly and landed sprawled in the center of the floor. Her attempt had set the ripples and water lily swaying. I stared at the rippling V's for a moment, and then I remembered what Gabriel had said about his magic tricks. *Misdirection.* He made people look where he wanted them to look.

I spoke slowly as I thought it all through. "What we need to do is get people noticing your dancing," I said, "rather than how tall you are."

Jade looked skeptical. "And how are you going to do that?" she asked.

I pointed to the ripples in Mom's hanging artwork. "We get people looking at your legs and not your head," I said simply.

"I don't think Mom's going to let me wear her artwork," Jade joked.

But I was too caught up in my idea to even smile. "Have you got an old practice skirt?" I asked.

"Sure," Jade said.

With Tutu trailing us, we went upstairs, where Jade pulled a gray skirt out of her dresser drawer.

"That'll work," I said, grabbing the skirt and turning to head back downstairs. "I'll be back in a bit."

I took the skirt into Mom's sewing room and sat down at the desk, sketching out a quick design. Then I opened the doors of the white armoire, searching for fabric scraps and scissors. I found some soft lavender fabric. *Perfect.*

I slid the gray skirt onto one of Mom's dress forms and sat down to start trimming strips of lavender fabric. When I had a pile of strips, I began *basting,* or loosely stitching, the strips onto the skirt in a series of V's. They looked like a formation of birds flying through the air.

When I was finished, I inspected the skirt. My heart was beating fast, as if I had just finished an intense dance routine. I slid the skirt carefully off the dress form and ran back upstairs to the bedroom, where Jade was sitting on the bed doing homework.

I nervously held up the skirt. *Would Jade be as excited about it as I was?* I wondered. "This is rough," I said, "but I'm hoping it will do the trick."

Jade cocked her head, as if she wasn't quite sure what to make of the skirt. She reached for it and then slid off her jeans and stepped into the skirt. Standing in front of our full-length mirror, she studied herself from different angles and twirled several times.

"Hmm, maybe," she said, smoothing her hands along the waistband of the skirt.

"Let's try your routine downstairs," I said, "where there's more room."

So we headed downstairs with Jade's laptop.

When she was ready, I started the music for her dance with the prince. I held my breath as Jade made her first turn. As she spun, the whirling V's of fabric acted like arrows, pulling my eyes down toward her legs. The skirt was working!

Jade was dancing as light and gracefully as ever. At least for now, she'd gotten back some of her confidence.

When she finished her routine, Jade looked down at her skirt. "It feels nice," she said, a pleased smile playing at the corners of her mouth. Then she lifted the edge of the skirt, and her expression changed. "Oh, no!"

I could see that some of the basted stitches had broken, and one of the lavender strips was hanging down. "Don't worry," I said quickly. "It's only basted together. Mom can fix it."

Just then, the front door creaked open. "It's only little old me," Dad called. A moment later, I heard him rummaging around in the hallway closet. I figured he'd done some holiday shopping before his gig. He always hid presents on a shelf there, assuming that covering them with a blanket would fool us. It hadn't worked since Jade was five and could drag a chair into the hallway.

A Magic Trick

Mom came home a minute later, and Dad started to shout frantically, "Stay outside! Don't come in!" Poor Dad.

When the gifts were safely hidden and Mom was allowed inside, she and Dad came into the living room together. Mom noticed Jade's skirt instantly. "Are you trying out a new costume?" she asked.

Jade glanced at me. "We were just trying out one of Isabelle's design ideas," she said hesitantly. I could tell that she was still afraid to tell Mom and Dad about her height problem.

Mom fingered one of the hanging strips of fabric. "I could help you sew it up," she offered.

"That'd be great," I said.

Dad looked thoughtfully at me. "What inspired that masterpiece?" he asked.

"Oh, I don't know," I said nervously. "It's sort of like when a new song comes to you."

I glanced sideways at Jade, and Mom folded her arms. "You girls are acting weird," she said. "Are you up to something? Tell me."

I saw Jade's cheeks redden, and I answered quickly, trying to defend her the way she always defended me. "It's nothing, Mom," I said. "We're handling it."

Jade smiled at me gratefully, but then she took a deep breath and confessed it all. "The truth is," she said, "I've got this problem. I'm taller than the prince in *The Nutcracker*, so sometimes people laugh when we dance together."

Mom sat down on the couch and pulled Jade toward her. "Oh, honey, is that what's been upsetting you?" she asked.

"And we didn't help any by talking about how much you've grown," Dad said with a shake of his head. "Sorry."

Jade played with a band of fabric on her skirt. "Isabelle came up with this idea," she said. "Maybe the skirt will make the audience look down rather than up, so they won't notice my height so much."

"Show me," Mom said, motioning toward the floor.

I started the music again so that Jade could dance. She did a few pirouettes and then asked anxiously, "So, what do you think?"

"I think it works!" Dad said. "Everybody's going to be paying attention to your dancing and not to the shrimp next to you."

Mom pressed her lips together thoughtfully

before she turned to me. "You're amazing, dear," she said. "The design of the skirt doesn't distract from Jade's dancing. It enhances."

I could tell by her expression, though, that she had more to say, so I lifted my eyebrows. "But?" I asked.

Mom tapped her chin. "Well, I think some lighter material would be good," she said. "I've got something perfect for that. And maybe we *ruche* the bands." Mom meant that she could sew pleats in the strips of fabric to give them ruffled edges.

I pictured the effect in my head, and I knew she was right. "Yeah, let's try that," I said.

"If you cut the material, I'll do the sewing," Mom proposed.

"Just help us fix the basting, Mom," Jade interrupted. "You're busy with the holiday fairs."

"Not *that* busy," Mom said.

Dad raised a hand. "Let's make it a family project," he said. "I can't sew, but I can cut material if you show me what to do."

Jade grinned at Dad. "Thanks," she said, and I could tell that all was forgiven between them.

Then Jade spun around again, watching her reflection in a mirror on the wall. She liked what

she saw so much that she did another spin, with all
of her old confidence. As the skirt settled about her,
she smiled at me in the mirror. That look was all the
thank-you I needed.

CHAPTER 9

The Toy Top

The next day when I was having lunch with Luisa and Gabriel in the school cafeteria, I told Luisa that I thought we'd solved Jade's problem.

"What problem?" Gabriel asked, popping a grape into his mouth.

"Some people were laughing because she was a little taller than her partner," I explained.

"If you can shrink her, that'd be real magic," Gabriel said. "I told you my secret. Now you tell me yours."

"Well, it's still sort of yours, Gabe, so thank you for that," I made a point to say. Then I described the skirt to him and Louisa, even sketching it out on a napkin. "It's helping Jade dance like her old self," I said, "but we can't really be sure it works until next Saturday. So keep your fingers crossed."

"Toes too," Luisa said.

She wanted Jade to succeed just as much as I did. I realized then how much pressure Jade was under. Sometimes it seemed as if the whole performance depended on her doing well. If Jade could conquer her problems, somehow the rest of us knew that we could, too.

Please let the skirt work, I wished, trying to cross my toes inside my shoes.

During the week, Jade and I practiced at home every night, taking turns watching each other so that we could give each other advice. In her new practice skirt, Jade seemed as graceful as ever. As for me? I was willing to settle for not "bowling over" any furniture.

In spite of all of our practice, Jade grew quiet as we walked toward the theater on Saturday. I didn't feel much like talking either—or even smiling. Maybe we were both too busy hoping that all of our hard work would pay off.

As we reached the stage door on the side of the HDC building, Jade reached for my arm to stop me. "Keep your mind on that toy top," she said in a soft but firm voice. "Remember what Jackie said. Shake off any mistakes. Everything just bounces off you while you spin: sticks, stones, insults, jokes." She swept her arm outward. "They just go flying off, right?"

"Right," I said. "You keep that in mind, too."

When we walked into Studio A and I saw Mr. Kosloff and Jackie Sanchez, I tried not to get nervous. Instead, I kept picturing that toy top whirling around and around.

The Toy Top

Jade had worn a long, puffy coat to protect against the chilly morning air. As she took it off, Luisa asked, "Is this the skirt Isabelle designed? I like it."

I glanced around, but no one else had noticed the skirt yet. And no one reacted to it during the party or battle scenes either. Without Paul dancing next to Jade, her skirt was just another rehearsal outfit.

But then came time for Jade to dance with Paul, her Nutcracker prince. I saw the ponytailed girl sitting next to the boy with glasses. They nudged each other as Jade danced a few early steps. When Paul finally stood up, I heard a giggle.

But as Jade and Paul began to dance, Jade's footwork was perfect. She moved, spun, and leaped with her usual grace. And there was no laughter now. Instead, everyone grew still as they watched her. Jackie Sanchez leaned over and whispered something to Mr. Kosloff, and he nodded at Jade. I felt warm, thinking that my skirt had helped her a little bit.

When Act One ended, Renata stood next to me and sighed. "I wish I were you so I could watch Jade dance all the time," she said dreamily.

"I'll tell her that," I said, wishing Renata would just go away.

Renata, though, stuck to me like a leech.

"But maybe I don't want to switch places with you after all," she said, her tone changing. "I mean, who wants to keep being reminded that you'll never be as good as your sister?"

I didn't need Renata to tell me what I already knew. I already compared myself too often to my sister.

Don't let her get to you, I told myself. *Shake her words right off.*

"Excuse me," I said, keeping my voice steady, "but I'd like to get ready for our routine now."

Renata smirked, but she left me alone.

Mr. Kosloff had been busy talking with Jackie and dictating notes to Bettina. But now he stood up to announce, "Let's take a ten-minute break." Then he crooked his finger at my sister. When Jade came over, I heard him ask, "Where did you get that skirt, Jade?"

"Isabelle designed it, and my family made it," Jade said proudly, turning to smile at me.

Mr. Kosloff had my sister turn around a couple of times slowly so that he could study the skirt from different angles. Folding his arms, he paused thought-fully, and then he waved me over, too. "Nice job with the skirt, Isabelle," he praised, and I felt a warm rush of pride in my chest. Then he pointed at the ceiling.

"Jade, will you go upstairs to wardrobe and ask for Margie? Tell her I want her to adjust your costume so that it has chevrons, like your practice skirt."

As Mr. Kosloff headed toward the door, Jade skipped over to my side and pulled me into a hug. "The skirt worked," she said, her voice muffled by my shoulder. "Thank you, Isabelle."

"It would just be an old practice skirt without your dancing," I reminded her.

But Jade shrugged off my words. She pressed her cheek against mine. "It's time for the toy top now," she said encouragingly. "Just remember: arms in, and spin so fast, you hum." She made a humming noise that I could feel—almost like Tutu purring.

Then Jade let me go so that I could begin visualizing the toys in the chest.

Most of the other dancers left the studio during the break, but some of my castmates stayed behind, like me. They took small half steps, their eyes staring off into the distance while they imagined their routines. Ms. Ferri leaned against the wall, her arms folded as she kept an eye on all of us.

I felt my cheek where Jade had touched me and thought about her humming. I was a top, perfectly balanced as I spun. The spinning was my armor.

Things bounced off. Nothing stuck. Not even Renata's words.

When Jade came back in with everyone else, Ms. Ferri took her place at the center of the floor and reached her arms like a mother hen so that her chicks could take shelter beneath them. I headed over with the other dancers and found my starting position.

At the first note of music, Ms. Ferri lifted and lowered her feet as she softly began to keep count: "One. Two. Three. Four. And five."

We began to move across the room like that giant crab. I tried not to think about how awkward and uncomfortable it was to be crouched down like this. Instead, I thought of how good it had felt to help my sister.

When we finally stopped, I scrunched down even lower and slipped away from under the imaginary skirt. I straightened and sprang upward, like Jack from his box. Lifting my head, I stretched my arms and legs outward as far as I could into a jeté. My landing was perfect.

As I neared Emilio, he began to stretch out his arms, and in my mind, I gave the toy top a twirl. I began my pirouette, arms in close and all my weight on one foot. Then I remembered Jade humming.

That would be the sound of the top spinning. I was a perfectly balanced toy.

As I circled away, I glimpsed Emilio's hands clutching at empty air. I was too fast. No one could catch me—not Agnes, not Luisa, not anyone. Not even Renata.

I danced back to Ms. Ferri. The others trailed behind me, but I would always be one step ahead of them.

I ducked down as if back under that imaginary skirt, moving around Ms. Ferri to make room for the others until she was surrounded.

She began moving her feet silently.

One. Two. Three. Four.

And then we were moving offstage.

When the piano music had finished, Luisa was the first to stand up. "That was perfect!" she said, giving me a hug.

It *had* felt perfect—well, almost perfect.

"You're doing great, Isabelle. Just remember to smile," Ms. Ferri pointed out. "Feel the joy."

It was easy to smile now, because I knew that I had danced well and made no mistakes. I knew that I *would* be the Gingerbread Girl, not Renata.

But could I repeat that performance? And could

I really pull it off before a live audience? *I hope, I hope, I hope* . . . I wished, still humming a little like that spinning toy top as I stepped off the dance floor.

CHAPTER 10

Mother Ginger's Skirt

I stared into the dressing-room mirror, and a Gingerbread Girl stared back at me. I laughed out loud.

My dress was gingerbread brown with big red plastic buttons. My cookie hat was round with a rim of white frosting. It was plastic, though, so as soon as I put it on my head, my scalp started to itch. And the hat was hot! I felt as if the top part of me really was a cookie, baking in an oven.

It was Sunday, the day of our dress rehearsal, and I couldn't wait to see Jade's costume and some of the others that I had helped to design.

Renata stepped in front of me, hogging the mirror. When Agnes complained from behind us, Renata half-joked, "You're just a maid. It takes a lot of work to make a duchess look like a duchess." She was putting on artificial lashes that were so thick and long, they reminded me of spider legs.

Jade had already done my makeup, including circles of rouge on my cheeks. When she had put on her own costume and makeup, she turned around so that Luisa and I could see. Luisa linked her arm with mine as she admired my sister. "Wow, Jade," was all she could say, and I couldn't agree more.

Wardrobe had put ruched V's—or *chevrons*, as

Mr. Kosloff had called them—on the skirt of Jade's costume, just as we had done on her rehearsal skirt. The sleeveless red costume was breathtaking. My sister had never looked more radiant, or more confident.

As Jade and I followed Luisa out of the dressing room, we couldn't help giggling. The fluffy tail of Luisa's furry fox costume waggled behind her with each step. Luisa looked back at us, and with her sly grin and pointy ears, she looked every inch the fox. She wriggled her tail even more as she gave a little hop.

When the three of us crowded into the wings, I saw that some of the boys in the party scene were wearing buttoned-down shirts and T-shirts now, just as I had suggested. And as a small mouse ran past, I saw that the head of her costume was cuter and more rounded, like the sketches I had created for Mr. Kosloff. He had taken my suggestions! My heart leaped in my chest. I could barely stand still.

"Let's check out the theater," I said to Luisa. We peeked around the heavy curtains and out into the theater beyond. The chandeliers on the ceiling burned like huge suns, and row after row of plush seats swept away from the stage like the waves of a red velvet sea. In the pit in front of the stage, a live orchestra was tuning its instruments.

As I stepped back into the wings, I saw a dancer in a colorful doll costume sliding her shoes back and forth in a pan of rosin on the floor. The rosin would keep her from slipping onstage. Next to her, another dancer rose *en pointe* several times, as if stretching out her feet or shoes. Another was checking the ribbons tied around her ankles.

"Isabelle! Luisa!" someone called. It was Agnes, letting us know that Ms. Ferri was looking for us. We followed Agnes to a space backstage where the rest of the cast had gathered.

Ms. Ferri was sitting on a chair, strapping her stilts onto her legs. A huge wig with auburn curls perched on her head. Seeing her wig made me think of my own costume, and I fought the urge to scratch beneath my cookie hat.

In heavy mascara, eye shadow, and rouged cheeks, Ms. Ferri looked like a painted doll. An elegant fan dangled on a strap around her wrist. From the waist up, she was dressed in a teal satin bodice, but from the waist down, she wore workout pants and running shoes. She looked like two different people who had been jammed together.

"Time to stretch," Ms. Ferri announced.

We did the best we could to warm up in our costumes. Agnes didn't have much trouble in her milkmaid outfit, but Renata's brocaded gown was stiff and heavy, so it made it hard for her to bend certain ways. Her tall, curly white wig nodded back and forth as she exercised.

Emilio's police outfit got my vote for the funniest. He had a high-domed helmet and a blue coat that reached down almost to his knees. His big fake mustache wiggled on its own, almost as much as Luisa's fox tail.

My costume, I'm sure, was the sweatiest and itchiest. My hair was already sticky beneath the hot plastic cookie hat.

When Ms. Ferri thought we were ready, she stood up on her stilts with the help of a stagehand. "And now, what every well-dressed giant wears," she said, glancing up at the large oval frame that held her skirt. The outer fabric was teal satin, like her bodice, but inside, the skirt was lined with plain white cotton material. Ms. Ferri held both arms up in the air as more stagehands started to lower the skirt over her.

Once the huge skirt had settled to the floor, the stagehands helped position it around Ms. Ferri's waist. To show us what it would look like to the audience, Ms. Ferri began to step sideways, the skirt bouncing up slightly on one side and then on the other like water lapping at the edges of a bowl.

"Now let's practice getting inside and out," Ms. Ferri said, beckoning us over.

Two of the stagehands lifted one end of the skirt, and we formed a line to file under it. As the hem settled back down to the floor, it was suddenly very dim. Only a faint light found its way through the layers of cloth. As roomy as the skirt might look from the outside, it was crowded for eight dancers in costume.

Above us, Ms. Ferri tapped the frame to get our attention. "I know it's a little stuffy inside," she warned, "but don't let that throw you off. Stay focused."

When Ms. Ferri pulled a drawstring, a panel rose on the front of her skirt. A thinner piece of material acted like a screen, and we slipped around that to step out of the skirt. In the crowded backstage area, we couldn't rehearse our full routine, but we could practice leaving and entering the skirt. So Ms. Ferri kept us busy making entrances and exits. We also practiced moving short distances back and forth in the skirt.

We stopped only when it was almost time for us to go onstage. Stagehands went ahead to clear chairs and props out of Ms. Ferri's path. She moved toward the stage slowly, like a satin-covered whale. When we reached the wings, I caught just a glimpse of Jade and Paul sitting on a throne upstage before I had to get inside the skirt with the others and wait.

As the first shivery notes of the tambourines began, Ms. Ferri's right stilt rose and sank slowly.

"One."

Her left stilt went up and fell.

"Two."

At "four," she took a step toward the stage and then stopped. We took our own step, moving slowly onto the stage. By now, we were used to the stilts themselves, but it was a little strange walking under the dim skirt instead of in a bright studio.

When Ms. Ferri halted and the panel went up, it was a relief to see the bright lights of the stage. But we'd no sooner left Ms. Ferri than Mr. Kosloff had us repeat our entrance and exit again.

And again.

And again.

It felt like riding in a racecar that had to halt every few yards. We never reached full speed or practiced our full routine, but at least I danced okay and didn't knock anyone over.

When we were back in the wings again, we were all glad to get out from under Ms. Ferri's skirt. "Coming?" asked Luisa, nodding toward the hall that would take us to the dressing room.

I was about to follow her when I realized that the next number was "The Waltz of the Flowers." I'd danced a shorter version of it at the Autumn Festival, so I wanted to see how real professionals did it.

"Do you want to stay and watch this with me?" I asked Luisa, and I was glad when she nodded yes. I gripped her arm excitedly as the flowers surged across the stage. They were all en pointe, and they seemed as light as dandelion fluff as they danced in intricate patterns and combinations of moves. The dancing was a lot more complicated than the routine I had done at our school show.

Luisa leaned her head against mine. "That's going to be you someday," she whispered to me.

"I hope so," I said. But these dancers seemed so flawless. I watched them carefully, waiting for one to make a mistake. "Everyone makes mistakes," Jackie Sanchez had said. But maybe she had just said that to make me feel better.

"The Waltz of the Flowers" finished without a hitch. That's when anxiety started to creep back into my mind. Sitting in this elegant theater, watching professional dancers in full costume onstage, everything felt so important and spectacular. *What if I make a mistake during our performance?* I wondered. *Worse yet, what if I'm the* only *one who makes a mistake?*

CHAPTER 11

A Timid Mouse

And then it was here.

The morning of our first performance, Jade and I rode the bus silently to the theater. I knew she was running through her dance images again just as I was—and Jade had a lot more to remember. But my stomach was so full of butterflies that I could barely remember what I'd had for breakfast an hour ago.

When we got off the bus and walked to the theater, I saw that the streets were jammed with holiday shoppers. People were lined up by the theater, waiting to pick up tickets to our show. They were expecting to see a holiday treat, not a holiday dud. I swallowed down the anxiety rising in my throat.

The clouds hung low overhead, and the bright bulbs of the marquee made sizzling noises as the damp air touched the hot glass. *Sizzling*. That was just how I was feeling inside.

When we entered the backstage area and passed by the dressing rooms of the company members, I saw jars, bottles, and makeup brushes lining the countertops beneath a row of lit mirrors. The mirrors illuminated the dark dressing rooms like little galaxies of stars.

A few minutes later, Jade was putting on my makeup—that last magical step that would help to transform me into the Gingerbread Girl.

Luisa sat in front of the mirror next to us. "Is Danny here?" I asked her.

"He got in last night," she answered. "He brought a couple of army buddies home with him. He's been bragging about me." Her right hand started to shake as she tried to brush on her eye shadow. "They're all out there with my parents."

Jade quickly took the brush away from Luisa. "Here, let me do that," she said. As Jade began to put on our friend's makeup, Luisa looked at me in the mirror.

She must have seen the nervousness in my face, too, because she asked, "Are you okay, Isabelle?"

I nodded. I couldn't tell Luisa what I was thinking inside. *Don't mess up today, Isabelle.*

Time went by too fast. The next thing I knew, I heard Bettina's voice over the loudspeaker. "Five minutes to curtain," she announced. "Partygoers to the stage."

"That's me," said Jade. She gave herself one last touch-up in the mirror.

"I'll come with you," I said. "Want to watch Jade with me, Luisa?"

"No, I'm going to stay here and go over my

routine," Luisa said nervously. "To the stars, Jade," she said, using our school's motto.

"To the stars, Luisa," Jade repeated with a smile.

As I followed my sister to the wings, I listened to the sounds from the theater. Because our performance was an afternoon matinee, there were a lot of children in the audience, so the noise was high-pitched and loud. I couldn't resist peeking from behind the curtain to look for my parents.

In front of me, the men in the orchestra wore dark suits, and the women wore white blouses with long black skirts or dress pants. Beyond them, from the front row of the theater all the way up into the balconies, I saw families filling the seats.

I couldn't see my parents in that mob, and now I wished I hadn't tried. When I'd danced at the Autumn Festival, that had been on the stage of our school auditorium. Now I was going to perform in a real theater. Make a mistake here, and I'd mess up *big-time*.

I tried to stay calm for my sister, who was about to go onstage, but as I turned toward her, I saw that she was already in her own little world. She took a deep breath, and as she let it out, her posture and expression changed. She was no longer Jade, but Clara. As her musical cue began, she danced onto the stage, where her stage family was already whirling about. Watching Jade dance, I knew one thing for certain: she belonged under those lights.

Suddenly I heard a little girl say, "I don't want to!" And then there was a *thump* from the backstage area behind me.

Turning around, I saw a little mouse had thrown the head of her costume onto the floor, where it was rolling around. I couldn't miss Addison's red hair and freckles. She was crying.

A larger mouse tried to calm her down. "But you *have* to," the older girl said, her voice muffled by the mouse head she was still wearing.

Addison crossed her arms and hung her head. "I'm going to mess up," she said through tears. "And everybody's going to laugh."

Bettina rushed over wearing a headset and a mike. "What's wrong, honey?" she asked, bending over beside her youngest mouse.

"I don't want to go onstage," Addison said.

"But everyone's counting on you," Bettina coaxed.

"I don't want to," Addison said. A fat tear

rolled down her cheek.

Bettina tried to convince Addison that every-thing would be okay, but that only seemed to make Addison cry harder.

I felt sorry for her. I knew just how she felt, so I went over and crouched beside her. "Hey, Addison. Remember me?" I asked. I wasn't sure she'd recognize me in my costume.

Addison studied my face for a moment. When she nodded, a few more tears broke free and trickled down her cheeks.

"Are you scared?" I asked gently. When Addison hesitated, I motioned to the other dancers. "Well, you know what? So are all the rest of us."

"Really?" Addison asked doubtfully.

"Dancer's honor," I swore. "Anyway, you couldn't mess up worse than I did in rehearsal a couple of weeks ago. I danced right into another girl and knocked her down. And do you know what she called me?"

Addison gave a little giggle. "What?" she asked.

I cupped my hand, as if I were whispering a great secret. "A bowling ball," I whispered in Addison's ear.

Addison laughed out loud.

"Shh!" said Bettina, holding a finger up to her lips. But she smiled at me.

I put my arm around Addison, and the padding in her mouse costume made a squishy noise. "It's okay to be scared," I said, remembering the advice that Jackie Sanchez had given me. "And it's okay to make a mistake. The important thing is to have fun, like you were doing the day we met. You danced the part of a blind mouse so well that Mr. Kosloff used you as an example for the other mice."

Addison smiled at the memory. "That was fun," she agreed, her big eyes shining.

I motioned to Jade and the other partygoers whirling around the stage. "Those dancers are having a lot of fun out there right now. Don't you want to go out and have fun with them?" I asked.

Addison bit her lip as she thought about it. Finally, she wiped her face with a big gray paw and nodded. She squatted down to pick up her mouse head.

I helped her put it on. "Let's both go out there today and have the most fun *ever*," I said to her. "Deal?" I reached out my hand and gave her paw a firm shake.

As Addison joined the other mice again, Bettina breathed a sigh of relief. "Thanks, Isabelle," she said in a low voice. "You were great with her."

When I stood up, I saw Jackie Sanchez watching us, too, from the wings. She grinned as she gave me a thumbs-up.

That meant more to me than a standing ovation. I was still feeling giddy as the partygoers came offstage.

Jade was glistening with sweat, her shoulders rising and falling as she tried to catch her breath. The audience would probably never realize how hard she worked to make her dancing appear so effortless. She looked as if she had just run a marathon in her party dress. I handed her a towel.

"Thank you," she said as she wiped her face and neck. Then she gave me a quick hug. "This costume feels magical," she said, motioning toward the red dress. "Isabelle, I'll never second-guess your designs again."

I grinned and gave her another hug. I hadn't even danced yet, and I was already flying high—first because of a thumbs-up from Jackie Sanchez, and now because my sister's performance had gone well, in part because of me.

Suddenly the floor beneath us began to vibrate, as if a train were thundering by. I heard the rumbling and creaking of machinery as a giant tree began to rise from the stage. I knew the audience would hear none of this, though, as the music of the orchestra swelled to cover up the rumbling of the gears.

As the tree finished growing, the oohs and aahs from the audience sounded like one giant sigh. "Mice, you're on," Bettina whispered.

Jade and I stepped to the side as the mice hurried onstage. Addison waved to me as she padded by. I tried to keep my eyes on her as she began to explore the house and the tree with the other mice. I had passed on Jackie Sanchez's advice to Addison, and she really seemed to be taking it to heart. She skipped and swaggered as if she were having the time of her life.

I only hoped that when it was my turn to go onstage, I could do the same.

CHAPTER 12

The Perfect Gingerbread Girl

The stagehands lifted one end of Mother Ginger's skirt. Leaning forward, I slipped inside with the other dancers. When the stagehands lowered it again, the bright lights from the stage made the fabric glow, as if we were inside a blue-green cloud.

When I wriggled my arms and shoulders to loosen up my muscles, Renata complained, "Quit elbowing me."

Ms. Ferri tapped the skirt frame for silence, and I felt the butterflies begin to whirl around in my stomach. So I tried to picture the toys in the chest. I didn't want to think about how cramped and dim it was inside this skirt or about how much my scalp itched beneath my cookie hat.

Finally, our music began.

Ms. Ferri's feet rose and fell, keeping time.

One.

My legs tensed.

Two.

Luisa's groping hand found mine.

Three.

I squeezed her fingers, wishing her good luck.

Four.

Overhead, the skirt began to bob back and forth as Ms. Ferri moved slowly toward the stage.

When the stilts clicked faintly against each other, I took a sideways step—and heard the soft whispering of ballet slippers as my castmates did the same.

One. Two.

Inside my stomach, the butterflies began whipping about as if in a hurricane.

Three. Four.

With each step, the skirt swayed like a ship in the ocean. Leaning over as I was, I felt like a giant trapped in a tiny boat as a storm churned up the waves around me.

We moved sideways until the stage lights shone through the teal fabric, and I could see the silhouette of the frame. The lights seemed to grow brighter and brighter as I followed the notes of our music. When Ms. Ferri stopped, I was ready.

The front panel of the skirt opened up, and I blinked through the thin second layer of fabric at the bright empty stage. The theater beyond the stage disappeared into darkness, and the stage looked like a raft floating beneath a starry night sky.

As I crept from beneath the skirt, I felt scared and excited all at once. I sucked in a breath of cool air, much cooler than the air had been beneath the skirt.

Then, straightening up, I took a couple of steps. Eagerly, I pictured the jack-in-the-box. I sprang into the air—and instantly heard the *wrong* musical notes.

Oh, no! I jumped too soon! The realization hit me like a brick wall. My worst fear had just come true.

When I landed, my mind suddenly went blank. Behind me, I heard the footsteps of the other dancers as they got into position. But which way was I supposed to go? What was I supposed to do?

In a panic, I glanced wildly around and saw Jade on the throne with Paul. Her hands were on her lap, but she moved them up and down as if they were hopping from spot to spot. It was a secret message meant for me.

Yes, the jack-in-the-box—my routine flooded back to me in one big wave. It felt as if I'd blanked out for hours, but from the music, I realized it had been only seconds. I still had a chance to save the scene, but I had to forget about my mistake—to shake it off, just as Jackie Sanchez had told me to do.

Turning, I saw Ms. Ferri as Mother Ginger. She was motioning for me to come back to her. I raised my hands upward, more in relief than in celebration. Then I shook my head at Ms. Ferri, just as I was supposed to.

The next moment, I pictured the jack-in-the-box again, and as my imaginary Jack popped upward and outward, I sprang away from Ms. Ferri.

Shake it off, I told myself again. *Just have fun. Feel the joy.*

I pictured Addison's tear-stained face breaking into a smile, and I began to dance just for her. I picked up the pace of my jumps, each of them stronger and higher and farther than the last. As I caught up to the right cue, I knew there was nothing to be afraid of. This sunny stage was our playground—meant for Addison and me.

I didn't just *hear* the notes of the orchestra; I felt them vibrate within me, like laughter bubbling up inside my chest.

On my next leap, I rose into the air with the musical notes, feeling as if we'd float up and up together until we could dance across the ceiling.

As my slippers thumped softly back down onstage, I told myself, *Next time, I won't come down. Next time, I'll fly on and on.*

Emilio gave me a big grin, as if he was having as much fun as I was. He licked his lips and rubbed his stomach. When he tried to grab me, I laughed as if he was the silliest boy in the world. There was no way a clumsy human could touch a cookie as clever and fast as me.

I held my arms just slightly away from my sides as I pictured the toy top. My legs had never felt stronger as I rose on one foot, and my turn had never been crisper as I spun out of Emilio's reach.

As his fingers grabbed the empty air, young, high voices began to laugh. And when I came neatly out of my spin, small hands began clapping frantically from all around the theater. Some little kids were rooting for this Gingerbread Girl to escape.

The laughter and applause encouraged my castmates, too. Agnes the Maid lunged at me as if she was starving. Renata the Duchess looked outraged when I didn't obey her commands. My Gingerbread Girl teased them all. No hand or paw or claw could touch me.

The only one who didn't try was Luisa the Fox. As I did my best to get her attention, I heard one little girl shouting at me not to do that.

When Luisa finally pounced at me, I pictured a toy top getting close to the edge of a table.

I have to spin away, I warned myself.

Raising my arms, I gave a kick that sent me into my pirouette. As I turned, I saw Mother Ginger

holding out her arms for me to come back to her so that she could protect me.

Beyond her, on the throne, Jade was giving me a big grin. From the way my cheeks were stretching, I knew I must be smiling just as broadly—and all on my own, without Ms. Ferri having to remind me.

The sight of Jade was all I needed. I sprang high in the air, not toward Mother Ginger but toward my sister sitting behind her. My feet barely touched the stage before I leaped again, feeling as light and free and happy as the music that swirled around me.

Suddenly I found my path blocked by Mother Ginger's skirt. As the panel flew up, I almost turned away. *No, it's too soon!* I thought. *I want to keep dancing!*

But from behind me, I could hear the others charging toward me. Even the Fourth of July and Christmas had to come to an end. So did this dance. *But there'll be another show,* I reminded myself. There was always the next show to look forward to.

Bending over, I slipped beneath the skirt. Crouching once again inside the glowing blue-green skirt, I moved away from the opening and made way for my castmates. I was Isabelle the dancer again, no longer the Gingerbread Girl.

I heard the other dancers panting as they

ducked after me into the skirt, one by one. As the last dancer, Emilio, entered, the flap dropped down again.

One. Two. Three. Four.

Ms. Ferri moved her feet in the same tempo as the music, and yet time seemed to speed by much faster now as we began our crab-walk offstage. When we reached the wings, out of sight from the audience, the stagehands lifted up one side of the skirt. Sweating and tired, we tumbled out and stood up. Every one of us was grinning from ear to ear. I gave Luisa a high-five, and pretty soon we were all high-fiving each other. Even Renata gave me a broad smile and a hand slap.

Luisa wrapped her arms around me. "I thought you had springs on your feet," she said with a laugh.

"A-plus performance, Isabelle," Ms. Ferri agreed. "You're the perfect Gingerbread Girl."

Perfect? It occurred to me suddenly that my performance had been anything *but* perfect. I had messed up my very first jump. But then I realized that Ms. Ferri was talking about how well I'd played my role as the Gingerbread Girl. Like Jackie Sanchez had said, a dance routine was about much *more* than doing the steps perfectly.

"Thanks," I said. "I had . . . I had *fun.*"

The applause was loud and enthusiastic during the curtain call, as Jade and the principal dancers took turns bowing and receiving bouquets of flowers.

I felt a little sad as the curtain closed for good. Beyond it, I heard seat cushions springing up and the murmur of voices as people began to leave the theater.

All around me, dancers were hugging one another. Mr. Kosloff appeared backstage and began drifting among the dancers, congratulating them. When he came to Luisa, he tweaked the ear of her costume and said, "There's my sly fox. Well done."

Then he grasped both my hands in his. "And here's my little jump-for-joy," he said warmly. "Excellent, excellent, Isabelle. And thank you so much for your help on the costumes. You've got a bright future ahead of you."

As Mr. Kosloff moved on, Luisa hooked her arm through mine. "Wow," she whispered in my ear. "Compliments on your dancing *and* your designs. You're batting two for two."

I grinned back at her. "Well, I bet your fox impressed Danny's friends, too," I said.

"I hope so," said Luisa, but without any of the

nervousness I saw before. She had danced well—she knew it. And her brother would be proud.

Luisa and I made our way through the crowd to Jade. Renata was already there, easing around Jade's roses to give my sister a quick, awkward hug.

As Renata made room for us, Jade threw an arm around me and hugged me tight, nearly crushing her roses. "There you are," she said. "It was always my dream to dance with you in *The Nutcracker*, and now it's really happened. You were just . . . wow!"

"So were you," I said, squeezing her back.

"I wish I could take a picture of you two," Luisa said. Suddenly she glanced over my shoulder, and her eyes widened. When Jade let go of me and stepped backward, her eyes were just as big as Luisa's.

When I felt someone tap my shoulder, I thought it must be another dancer wanting to congratulate me. But when I turned around, I found myself face to face with Jackie Sanchez.

"Hi, Isabelle," she said. "What a wonderful Gingerbread Girl! I could tell you had fun out there. Your leaps had such joy. And your happiness was contagious. You were having fun, and so the other dancers did, too."

"Thanks," I managed to say.

"I also liked how you kept your cool and calmed that little mouse down before she had to go on," she added.

"Well, I kind of knew how she felt," I said truthfully.

"I think you're just the kind of person I need for a pet project of mine," Jackie said, raising her eyebrows. "What do you think? Will you be in my show?"

Me? Dance with Jackie Sanchez? My mouth dropped open, but no sound came out.

This was so far beyond anything I had ever dreamed of. Jackie Sanchez was famous all over the world for her dancing, and I had just performed for the first time in a real theater. I didn't belong on the same stage as her.

Jackie smiled patiently as she waited for my answer, but my tongue felt like a lump of lead.

As usual, my big sister came to my rescue. Putting her hand on my cookie hat, Jade forced me to nod my head up and down.

"My sister," Jade announced, "would be glad to."

Letter from American Girl

Dear Readers,

Isabelle finds a creative way to use her talent for fashion design to help her sister, Jade. Here are the stories of some real girls who also have a knack for fashion—and helping others.

Read about a trio of friends who opened a sewing and mending center in their school library; a knitter who sold her designs to raise money for someone in need; and two girls who created a magazine to share fashion tips with others.

As you read these stories, you'll learn some tips for how to follow *your* passion for fashion, too.

Your friends at American Girl

A Sewing Club

Learning to make bags and skirts from recycled fabric was fun for members of one school sewing club. But those projects were just the start of their effort to be "sew green."

It takes energy for a factory to make and ship a new piece of clothing, and it costs money for a person to buy it. "We knew that throwing things out wastes energy and money," says one club member, Michelle W., age 11. When club members realized they could help their Illinois school to be more earth-friendly, they opened a

Aida, Michelle, and Sunny

mending center in the school library. Students and staff could drop off items that needed to be fixed, and club members would do the work for free. "So, instead of buying a new pair of jeans, you could keep the ones you've been wearing," says Aida S., age 11.

Recycling tips:

Before you throw away a stained or torn piece of clothing, think about ways to reuse it. T-shirt embellishments, jeans pockets, and buttons make great craft supplies. Ask a parent for help removing them from ruined clothing.

Club members mended lots of jeans, as well as shirts, backpacks, socks, sweaters, and even puppets used in a prekindergarten classroom. The club was always busy with mending projects, and people's reactions made the club's effort worth it, says Sunny L., age 11. "People were really happy and excited that their clothes were fixed."

Sunny and Aida work to re-cover some chairs.

Michelle and a newly repaired puppet

A Knack for Knitting

Phoenix B., a 14-year-old Virginia girl, started a business designing knitted clothing and accessories such as sweaters, arm warmers, dancewear, and bags. It all started when she entered a shawl that she had designed in an art show, and she won first place. When everyone wanted to buy the shawl, Phoenix realized that she could turn her hobby into a business. She designed more shawls in different shapes and sizes and started selling them in stores and on her website.

What advice would Phoenix give to girls who want to learn how to knit? She says girls can go to a yarn store and ask about knitting classes. "The first thing you knit will look like my first hat—homely and frumpy, something that you will put in your drawer and hope that nobody sees. But don't get discouraged," she says. "The more you knit, the better you'll get!"

Phoenix's fingerless gloves are almost as soft as her dog, Galina.

Phoenix created this bag to raise money to buy a wheelchair for a girl who needed one.

Design Doodles

Emily G., age 11, gives this tip for creating a sketchbook for fashion-design doodles: "Glue a piece of colored paper to the front of the journal. Use craft glue to attach buttons, fabric, and ribbon scraps. Add your name with glitter puffy paint. Let dry. Now start designing your own line of clothing!"

Catwalk Creations

Laura D., age 12, and her friend Emma thought it would be fun to create a fashion magazine for their classmates to read. They named it *Catwalk Magazine* and came up with some great features, including fashion debates, tips, and contests. Now many people enjoy reading their magazine, and the fashion-forward friends are proud of their work!

Emma P. and Laura D.

About the Author

Laurence Yep is the author of more than 60 books. His numerous awards include two Newbery Honors and the Laura Ingalls Wilder medal for his contribution to children's literature. Several of his plays have been produced in New York, Washington, D.C., and California.

Though *The Nutcracker* was a regular holiday treat for Laurence as a boy, it was his wife, Joanne Ryder, who really showed him how captivating and inspiring dance can be with her gift of tickets to the San Francisco Ballet. Their seats were high in the balcony, yet they were able to see the graceful, expressive movements of the dancers far below.

Laurence Yep's books about Isabelle are his latest ones about ballet and a girl's yearning to develop her talents and become the dancer she so wishes to be.